WALKER ON AIR

A huge exultation possessed him, a feeling of power, of freedom; the rapture of flight and all its attendant miracles were finally his. Finally, after years of studying, observing, and crashing, he could fly back to Britain and rain revenge on the man who had stolen his kingdom and ravished his wife.

Who was this Walker on Air? Was he the fore-runner of our modern superheroes? A mythic hero like Arthur and Lancelot? Or was he a real per-son, the first man to hang-glide, riding the winds thousands of years before our time?

Woven from threads of legend and a universal dream, BLAEDUD THE BIRDMAN is a shim-mering tale of magical intrigue, heroic quest, and a fabled prince who stunned the civilized world by walking on air.

Other Avon Books by
Vera Chapman

BLAEDUD THE BIRDMAN

VERA CHAPMAN

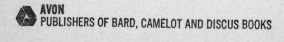

AVON
PUBLISHERS OF BARD, CAMELOT AND DISCUS BOOKS

AVON BOOKS
A division of
The Hearst Corporation
959 Eight Avenue
New York, New York 10019

First Avon Printing, February, 1980

Contents

Foreword

We first hear of Blaedud, or Bladud (I prefer "Blade-ud" to "Blad-ud" simply for the sake of euphony), in the pages of Geoffrey of Monmouth, who wrote in the twelfth century. "Everybody knows" that Geoffrey of Monmouth was a liar, or so it used to be said. Among other things he was said to have "invented" King Arthur for political ends. But modern researchers have begun to reconsider Geoffrey of Monmouth and King Arthur—and why not Blaedud? Perhaps under all that romantic smoke there actually was some fire?

This is what Geoffrey tells us, as translated by Aaron Thompson in 1718.

> "Next succeeded Blaedud (Hudibras's son) and reigned twenty years. He built Kaerbadus, now Bath, and made hot Baths in it for the Benefit of the Publick, which he dedicated to the Goddess Minerva . . . The Prince was a very ingenious Man, and taught Necromancy in his Kingdom, nor left off pursuing his Magical Operations, till he attempted to fly in the upper Region of the Air with Wings he had prepared, and fell down upon the Temple of Apollo in the City of Trinovantum, where he was dashed to Pieces."

The other principal legend about Blaedud, that of the pigs, seems to go back to folk memory. But both these tales, the wings and the pigs ("Pigs might fly"??) have been repeated and elaborated over centuries by both the naive and the learned.

I am infinitely indebted to Mr. Howard C. Lewis, who in

7

his *Bladud of Bath* (published privately in 1919 and publicly in 1973) has made a comprehensive collection of the various records, traditions and literary versions of the Bladud story. I trust that my retelling of the plain tale is no worse a travesty than, say, that of Michael Drayton or John Wood.

As I write, the national press acclaims Ken Messenger, who has "hang-glided" across the Channel in twenty minutes. In these days we have safer methods of flying, for anyone who does not have a Bird-Woman to protect them; still, I would invoke her protection on all who attempt that hazardous sport.

VERA CHAPMAN

Prologue

The man who was called Brutus of Troy raised his sword above the distant landscape below and plunged it into the earth.

"Here" he said, "I will build the New Troy."

The hill was open, sunny, treeless and clothed with heather, where the bees made drowsy music in the noon. Below, a long way below, the land dropped into softly sloping plains. Small streams, catching the light, ran here and there, all downward to the north-east, and eventually merged into a great river, seen far off.

"A royal city," he said, "all over the great plain, under these hills, right to the river and beyond."

"So big a city, my Lord?" questioned the man who stood behind him bearing his shield. "But there has never been a city as big as that. Not even Rome . . ."

"It shall be greater than Rome, some day," he said with a visionary look. "Prepare the altar."

The half-dozen men with him began to build an altar of turf, cut from the ground where they stood.

How long ago had they come from Troy? Nobody could tell for certain, but many generations back from Troy they had certainly come, by way of Rome. The great and good Aeneas, with his old father and his little son, had survived the fall of the great city, and wandered by way of Carthage to Italy. There the sons, or maybe the grandsons, of Aeneas had built Rome, and then one of them, who was called Brutus, had gone on his travels again, as the stars and the sun led him. Always as the sun led him between mid-

9

summer and the autumn equinox, and by night it was the Bear that led him on, as it turned round a point that never altered, the north-west. And Brutus and his followers had paused on the way, and settled for a time, and he had died, and another Brutus had succeeded him, and after a while they had gone north-west again, and so on, and so on . . .

There were never many of them, though the tribe increased where they settled, and each time a new Brutus went out there would be perhaps twenty warriors, and nine or ten women, and always one or two priests. The priests belonged to a very old line, and wore long white robes, and made sacrifices to the Father and to the Mother and to the spirit that lived in the oak trees. They had secret magic rituals, which they taught only to their successors, and it was said that they knew the art of writing, that they had learnt it from the men who lived in Etruria before the Romans came; but they never wrote their secrets. It was the priests who knew how the sun and the stars moved, and marked out the times and seasons, and proclaimed the time and the direction of the setting-out—always to the north-west.

At first, when they left Italy, the tribe had to cross great snowy mountains. Later they came to wide forests that ran on and on and to great rivers which they followed. Then at last (in the lifetime of *this* Brutus) they reached the sea. Here they wondered if their rovings were to cease, but the priest led them on "Still go north-west," the stars told him. So they made themselves coracles and crossed the sea. A green and beautiful land opened up before them, and a wide river took them in. Here Brutus stepped ashore upon a great stone, and his little company followed him. He marked that stone with mystic symbols and set it up.

"Here shall be a town," he said, and so in after years it was. A portion of his company stayed behind, and the rest went on.

Turning back down another river, they came to the sea again, and here was a settlement of little dark men, who were glad to see them because they lived in fear of a giant. So Brutus stood on the clifftop and called the giant to come out and wrestle with him.

The giant was one of an older race of folk, perhaps the last of them. He was twice the size of any of the little dark people, and his hair was rusty red and grew all over him. His arms were so long that his hands touched the ground as he walked, with his knees bent, shuffling. His jaw was huge and bony, and his eyes small and sunk in great bony sockets, and he seemed to know no language. He lived on stolen cattle and murdered men. The people called him Corin, which seemed to mean Cerunnos, the kindly horned god of the beasts both wild and tame, whom they had worshipped before they crossed the seas. But to the Trojans he was in no way like their god.

So Brutus wrestled with the giant upon the clifftop, and though the giant was so vast Brutus had greater skill. He broke the neck of the giant and hurled him into the sea. And so, leaving another part of his band to settle there, and to trace in pebbles the story of the fight on the clifftop, Brutus and his remaining company moved, still northward but now towards the east.

And now the sun rose over the heights of New Troy, and Brutus's men led forward a great white bull and bound it on the altar of turf, and Brutus with his great sword gave the stroke of sacrifice and the blood ran down to give life to the land.

"This shall be the Land of Brutus," he said, "and this place is Troia Nova."

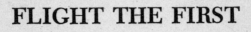

FLIGHT THE FIRST

Birds and Bird-Woman

"Prince Blaedud," said the Druid, "you are not attending."

"Oh, I'm sorry, honoured Syweddyd," said Blaedud, and forced his attention back. But the birds—the birds—they were circling and calling above his head, and he had to look back at them.

Ten years old, a red-haired thickset boy, with round pebble-blue eyes in a rosy sunburnt face, he sat obediently enough on the low stone seat in the sunshine, but below him he could hear the sea and above him those birds, those birds . . .

"Prince Rud," said the Druid to the next pupil, "what are the three essentials of learning?"

Rud, a tow-haired cheerful boy with a mischievous face, answered glibly enough.

"To worship the Gods, to do no evil, to exercise fortitude."

"Very well answered," said Syweddyd. "Now, Prince Blaedud, the three points of good discipleship?"

"Keen observation . . ." began Blaedud, but the words faded out on him. Those birds! They were gulls, the black-headed ones that put their black caps on for the summer, and they were wheeling and dipping between the clear blue sky and the clear blue sea. Sweeping and veering in incredible freedom, hovering down with claws outstretched to the sea, and then off and away, with hardly a wingbeat . . . If he watched them long enough the Bird-Woman would come.

She had come to him first when he was very small and

very lonely. Seven years old he was, and they had taken him from his nurse and handed him over to the men, because that was the custom. And he had toothache and nobody cared.

Not that he had ever known his mother—she had died at his birth—but his father, King Hudibras, had two other wives, as well as several women slaves, and they had all looked after him, and one of the women slaves had nursed him and been all the mother he had had. But now, he was told, he must leave the women and go with the men. So he lay in the dark with his aching tooth and cried. And suddenly she was there.

She was all soft warm feathers, with wide wings that wrapped him round, and a lovely kind mothering face that bent above him.

"Come," she said, "we are going to fly," and she clasped her long-fingered hands round him as easily as if he had been a little swaddled baby, and gathered him into the warmth of her feathered bosom. His aching face sank gratefully into the softness, and she lifted her great pinions and they flew up into the sky. Whether they went out of the door, or through the little round unglazed window, or just clean through the stone walls, he could not say. But in a minute they were up into the dark blue night air, soaring high above the treetops. She held him so firmly that he had no fear and presently managed to turn his head and look below him.

They were far, far up, over the hills. Below him he could make out the edge of the cliff, on the island where the College of Princes was, a little circle of thatched roofs, close to the stone circle that was the temple. There was the sea, all round the island, and the moon making a long path across it. All was wonder and peace. Far, far into the night they flew, over mountains and rivers and lakes. His eyes drooped and a delicious sleep came over him.

When he woke in the morning, the toothache was gone and the tooth lay beside him on his pillow. In a month or so he had a fine new one in its place. But the memory of that night stayed with him.

He might have thought it just a dream like other dreams, but she came again, long before the new tooth had grown, and again they flew together. She told him, "This is just till you can fly on your own. Some day I shall not need to hold you. You will fly."

"What, shall I fly like you?"

"Yes, you shall fly. Remember that." How could he forget it?

"Yes, Prince Blaedud? Keen observation . . . ?"

"Keen observation and . . . and . . ."

His eyes were back on the gulls wheeling above him. It was pleasant out there on the grass, in front of the circle of stone huts that was the College of Princes. There was a ring of tree stumps set in the grass for the pupils to sit on while the Druid teachers taught them, under the eye of heaven. When it rained they had to go into Syweddyd's hut, which was large as such things went, and sit round the fire under the smoke-hole, but there were not many days bad enough for that. The hut circle looked down over the sea on the island's flank and there were no other buildings for leagues and leagues around, only the sheer drop over the sea and to the northward a strip of shallow water and then the mainland. For the College of Princes was built on the island they called Sea-Foam, that later the Romans called Vectis.

"Keen observation and . . . and . . ."

"Well, go on. Keen observation . . . you then, Prince Dardan." Dardan was long limbed, long faced and dark. He answered readily enough.

"Keen observation, retentive memory . . ."

"Oh yes, retentive memory," said Blaedud all in a rush, "and yes, reverence for truth . . . Oh, honoured one, I *didn't* have retentive memory—I'm sorry—because I was observing."

"Observing *what*, young Prince?" said the Druid, frowning like schoolmasters in all ages.

"Observing the flight of the birds, honoured ancient one," said Blaedud.

"Ha, that nonsense again," said Syweddyd. "You must not let your mind wander, young Prince. You have to learn the Triads."

Another Druid was watching at the door of the large hut, rather older than Syweddyd, very grey, with twinkling blue eyes.

"Syweddyd, my friend," he said, "it seems to me the young prince has shown the three essentials in himself—keen observation, certainly, and regard for the truth as well. Let us see if he has also retentive memory. Shut your eyes, Prince Blaedud. Now tell me—what kind of birds?"

"Black-headed gulls, honoured ancient one, with their black caps on for summer."

"How many?"

"Oh, forty, I should think."

"And what did you learn of their manner of flight?"

"Oh, they lean against the wind—when they go upwards, it's into the wind they go, and to go down they turn, and they tilt their wings to go this way and that. They sit on the sea and when they rise they thrust themselves against the air with their feet . . ." He opened his eyes and turned his intense gaze on the older Druid. "Honoured Ceredig, tell me, do please tell me—why can't we fly like birds?"

Ceredig laid an affectionate hand on the boy's shoulder, and placed him on one of the log seats by his side.

"Oh, little piglet!" he said. "What thoughts you little piglets do have! Yes, you too, Prince Rud and Prince Dardan. Children, it's not in nature for men to fly. Prince Rud, now tell me, what are the four Elements?"

"Earth, air, fire and water."

"Prince Dardan, what creatures go on the earth?"

"Men, and beasts, and creeping things."

"And in the water?"

"Fishes and whales and the great sea-serpents."

"And in the air?"

"Birds and all insects and the Messengers of the Gods."

"And in the fire?"

"Only the salamander."

"Rightly answered. Now, you see, Prince Blaedud, the place for men and beasts is on the earth."

"But sir—" the boy's eagerness got the better of his awe of the teacher—"Sir—there's the flittermouse. He's a mouse, not a bird, and he flies."

The Druid shook his head. "Even the flittermouse is of the nature of the air, and therefore a bird."

"But I caught one, sir—it lay on the ground, and I looked at it and felt it, and it had fur on it, not feathers, and round ears and a tail like a right mouse, and its wings were made of skin stretched between its fingers and its toes."

Syweddyd was frowning, and now he broke in.

"Prince Blaedud, it is not seemly or wholesome or holy to touch things like that. You must not do it. Now, come—learned Ceredig, by your leave—we turn to the genealogies. Prince Blaedud, turn your mind away from the birds, lest you grow as flighty and light as a bird, and tell me the generations between Brutus of Troy and your royal father."

Blaedud began readily enough,

"Brutus of Troy, Locrine, Guendollen the Queen, Madden, Mempricius, Ebraucus, Brutus Greenshield, Leil, and our royal father Hudibras . . ."

"How many is that?"

"Eight kings and one queen."

It was the dark-faced Dardan's thoughts that were running off now. Guendollen the Queen—one was always curious about her. A beautiful woman, they said, but bad. Guendollen who had made war on her husband and pushed him from the throne, who had drowned her stepdaughter, the innocent Sabrina, out of jealousy—an interesting woman, but bad. One remembered Guendollen.

"Well answered, Prince Blaedud." The old teacher's long grey face was frostily benevolent. "Now you, Prince Rud."

Rud rattled off the list glibly. He made two slips and Syweddyd stopped him and corrected each one.

"Now remember," he said, "let these be impressed upon your memory, with the Triads and the rest of the holy wisdom, for it is the record of our people. On your memory it depends. Teach it to your sons and your sons' sons, for if you forget it, or they do, it is lost. It will have no memorial otherwise."

The three boys thought this over in serious silence.

"Honoured ancient one," said Blaedud, "is it then that this is the only record—our memories?"

"Yes, my son, the only record. Therefore hold it fast."

"But why not . . . could it not be written down?"

Syweddyd gasped.

"Written down? *Written down?* Great Gods . . ."

He turned away, shaking his head. Then composing himself, stroking his long beard, he said,

"My son, to write these things down would be a great

wickedness. First, because it is against the Law. And second, that if such things were written down, the secrets of the Wisdom would no longer be safe. They must not be known to any but the chosen—the Chief's sons and the Druids' sons. If they were written, on skins or on bark, on stone or on metal, why . . . anyone who knew how to read might find them and read them! Anyone!"

"But, honoured ancient one," put in Rud, who now seemed as interested as Blaedud, "surely there are many things—such as the genealogies—that everyone ought to know?"

"Certainly not!" said Syweddyd, frowning so that the dark lines on his face stood out portentously. "Not the lists of the Kings nor the least little fragment of the Wisdom. Look to it, and remember you are all three vowed to secrecy."

"But wouldn't it be better," Blaedud persisted, "if more people were wise?"

"No, it would not," pronounced Syweddyd. "Prince Blaedud, you have some strange ideas, and I do not think them good. You must not infect Prince Rud and Prince Dardan with them. See to it."

He twitched his white head-veil forward over his face and walked away. From the doorway of the big hut, Ceredig watched, his eyes bright, a smile playing about his lips. He caught Blaedud's eye.

"Three things go where they will, and none can stop them," he said. "The wind, the thoughts of a boy, and the spirit of knowledge."

That night the Bird-Woman came again. She lifted him effortlessly, and they floated high, high over seas and continents. They looked down on places that Syweddyd had never taught him about. And then she let him fly a little beside her, under the beating shadow of her great wings. They flew low, so that they could see the beauty of the rivers and the valleys. At last he began to feel he was a bird. Then among the rushes by a great river's side he saw something white and golden. He stooped towards it—a white bird, sitting on a nest. A little smooth rounded head, the soft white wings spread below and around her, the swelling white breast—the bird of all birds. With a glad

20

cry he hastened towards her, and then felt the great wings above and around him troubled and angry.

"No, no!" cried the Bird-Woman. "Not there, not there. Death, death, death!" and her strong hands clasped his and held him again, restraining him. But he could see now that the beautiful thing below him, sitting so peaceful and settled upon her nest, was not a bird but a girl. A white shining golden-haired girl. He struggled against the restraining hands.

But the Bird-Woman held him fast and whirled up and away. "Never, never, never!" he heard her saying. "Not for you. Not that one, or you will never fly." She carried him on through the sky, and in the dreamy drift of scene after scene he forgot the moment of struggle and anguish, and let himself go in the pleasure of that long wandering. When he woke, he did not remember the white bird on the nest. Not at that time, not till long afterwards.

Fledglings

"Come through this way," said Blaedud, and led the other two boys through a gap in what seemed like solid gorse bushes and brambles. The hot sun of harvest time beat down on them, and drunken wasps reeled among the dripping juice of the blackberries. The boys found themselves in a close circle of brambles where there seemed no way out.

"Now. Before we go on, you must swear."

"What must we swear, Blaedud?" said Rud. "You didn't say anything about swearing."

"You must swear to keep the secret of this place and of what we do in it."

"But what must we do?" Dardan, the youngest, followed Rud's lead.

"Put your hands on my knife—it's a flint one, not made by a smith but by one of the old people, so it's extra holy—and say 'I, Rud, son of Hudibras, promise to you, Blaedud, son of Hudibras, that I will never reveal the secrets of this place.'"

Rud obediently repeated the words.

" 'And if I do, may the Old Woman run after me as she ran after Gwion, and cut my throat and devour me.' "

"Oh . . . must I say that? It's rather horrible . . ."

"Yes, you must."

The words were duly repeated.

"And now kiss your finger, touch your own knife with it, draw your finger across your throat, and say 'See it's wet, see it's dry, cut my throat if I tell a lie.' "

In fear and trembling Rud did so. Then Dardan did the same.

"Now come through here," said Blaedud, and pulled away a loose branch of gorse, revealing a narrow tunnel. They scraped through—although their skins were sunburnt and tough, the brambles and gorse prickles scored them nastily, and the goatskins which were their only kind of garment gave them only a minimum of protection.

"Here," complained Dardan, "I'm being clawed to bits and there's a horsefly after my blood. I'd sooner wrestle with a cat."

"Oh, come on," said Blaedud, "we're nearly there. Now —look!"

They emerged on the lip of a dell, deep and secluded. A stream had hollowed it out over centuries and trickled down some twenty or thirty feet below, to a bottom of dense undergrowth. Halfway down it had worn out a shallow cave and Blaedud led the way to this. He climbed down very quietly, almost as if there was something in the cave he was afraid of disturbing.

"This is my magic study-place," he said. "Before you go in, you must say 'Wings.' "

" 'Wings,' " each one said with the solemnity of a game or a ritual.

Inside the cave, which was of yellow sandstone and full of light, Blaedud removed a piece of rough cloth. Under it was a board on which was nailed a dead bat and a dead crow, their wings outspread. Behind was a heap of various kinds of feathers, and an odd-looking contraption of sticks, cloth and ropes.

"You see?" he said. "First I'm trying to find out how a bird flies—how its wings are made up, how it moves them, and everything about it. Then look at this. I'm trying to make wings. Why *shouldn't* a man have wings? They fly along the sea with sails—old Syweddyd said nothing about ships in his list of sea creatures! Just like wings, the sails of a boat are, only they just skim along, they don't go up. Why not? Why not?"

The question seemed to be addressed to Dardan, who answered rather blankly,

"Because a boat's heavy."

"Heavy? Why shouldn't it be made lighter? A swan's heavy—have you ever lifted a dead swan, or a dead goose come to that? They don't weigh just nothing, and yet they lift up off the surface of the water and fly. Now come on and let's see what we can do with this."

They busied themselves about the cave. First they explored the bottom of the dell and found that it was mostly deep soft brushwood, but they cut bracken and piled it high, to make a soft surface to land on. Then Dardan was stationed below while Rud, at the top of the dell, bound on to Blaedud's shoulders the clumsy contraptions of sticks, cloth and stretched leather. At his word, he gave him a vigorous push over the edge.

Blaedud flapped the great objects helplessly, and fell like a stone, fortunately on to the prepared mattress of bracken and brushwood. The boys shouted, half in excitement and half in panic. Dardan caught him as he fell and got a swipe across the face from one of the "wings," which made his nose bleed.

"No good that time," said Blaedud. "Try again."

Again and again they tried it, until the sun dipped and it was time to go home, Dardan with his bloody nose, Rud with a black eye, and Blaedud with a twisted ankle, and all three of them covered with scratches.

"We'll have to say we've been fighting," Blaedud said, "and get a scolding from old Syweddyd."

So they went on day after day, trying this way and trying that, and miraculously breaking no bones. Blaedud never told them about the Bird-Woman, but he felt that she kept them from coming to any serious harm. But if he had told them about her, he was convinced that it could have brought disaster.

The Wedding Day

The three boys were the sons of King Hudibras, but not by the same mother. Blaedud was not only the eldest but the son of the lady queen, the chief wife. He was therefore the High Prince. But the other two, being sons of the King's wives, were princes too. There were also sons of concubines, not to mention daughters of concubines, but these were of little account. All went to make up the population of the great sprawling "royal house," half fortress and half homestead, that lay on the top of the hill where Brutus of Troy had founded his Troy-Novant. Nine monarchs had come and gone since that time, by rough reckoning between two and three hundred years, and the way of life had changed very little, save that the tribe was no longer a wandering tribe, but had settled and built round houses of wood and clay on stone foundations, and had spread their flocks over the high hill pastures and ploughed a few fields, not very deep, in the soft soil below the hills, and there grew grain for bread and ale. Down below, along the river, a few families lived too, and caught the abundant fish. And where the river widened to the sea ships sometimes came, with news many months old of the great world afar off, of Gaul and Rome and Greece, and with rich and strange things to trade for furs and pearls and dogs and slaves.

Houses were more solid than the tents in which Brutus's men had lived, though even the King's palace was no more than a group of huts, larger and smaller, connected by paths, with one hut, as large as a roof could be made to cover, for assembly. Furnishings were almost as simple as they had been at least two hundred years before, and clothes had not changed much either. The summers were long and hot, so the boys (like our three princes) needed nothing more than their scraps of goatskin tied on with thongs, but for more formal wear, and in colder weather, the usual dress for everyone was much the same, a long piece of coarsely woven woollen cloth, no wider than an arm's stretch but of any length, girt around the waist like a sketchy sort of kilt, with the end slung over the shoulder in the manner of a plaid. But the ingenious restless minds of the women, of course, were always finding different ways of arranging this, as well as experimenting with dyes— madder and woad and saffron and the juices of berries. And those that were very rich or great or fanciful might sometimes get some precious stuffs from overseas, dyed scarlet or purple or bleached snow white and embroidered by cunning hands in distant countries.

And one of those robes was now being carefully draped over the tall body of Prince Blaedud. Seven years had gone by since we watched him and his brothers in the College of Princes. He was now eighteen, and his father had sent for him to return from the Druids' settlement on the Isle of Foam to the stronghold on the hill above the river Tamis, to the King's court at Caer Troia.

The three boys had travelled together, slowly, on their stocky native ponies, their long legs dangling down only just clear of the ground. Nobody had told them why they had been sent for. On arrival, Blaedud had been separated from the other two, and after a night's rest the house-servants were arraying him in quite unaccountably splendid garments—flaming scarlet wool, caught up on the shoulders with loops and pins of gold.

The leather curtain that served for a door was flung back and there stood his father, King Hudibras, an over-whelming figure of a man, ruddy and sandy, broad shoul-dered and enormously fat. His red-gold hair, a little faded into grey, fell massively on his shoulders, and his beard spread out like the rays of the sun. He was draped in purple, that billowed royally around him, and he was liber-ally adorned with gold, a heavy gold collar which his beard almost hid, bracelets of gold all the way up his arms, clank-ing as he moved, and a gold coronet on his head, with one round red stone above his brows.

"Blaedud, my son!" He swept down upon him like a tidal wave of gold and purple. "My boy, this is a great day for you and for me. Do you know why you are here?"

"No, father," said Blaedud, feeling very small indeed and rather alarmed.

"Then listen, boy, listen and learn. This is none other than your wedding day. You are to be married."

The king beamed at him like a summer sunrise.

"Married, father? What, me? Me, father? Married?"

"I said married. Yes. Just that. Look, boy, you're eighteen and over. It's time and high time. You are my heir, the ninth from Brutus. Now it's your turn to get someone to carry on after I am gone. You're a man now. Before you go into some battle and get killed, what? Oh, I know there's Rud and Dardan, but you're the High Prince, and I want your sons, yours and no others, to be kings of this land and tribe after me."

"Oh, yes, father, but . . . the lady? Who is she?"

"Eh, who is she? Your wife, of course, that I've provided for you. The mother of your lawful sons, nobody else."

"But who . . . ?"

"Oh, yes, of course, you'll want to know who she is. Why, she's the daughter of the King of Ikkeni. One of his daughters, he has two. The elder, of course. Oh, a very nice girl, and suitable for you. Her name? Why now, there's the two of them, and which is it? I don't know. One's Guendollen and the other's Elen. There you are—Elen or Guendollen, whichever it is. They'll both be here. Oh, yes, one of them's dark, like all the Ikkeni, the other's fair, like her mother, who was one of the Belgae. Well, what's the matter, young fellow? You don't look too pleased."

"It's rather sudden," said Blaedud, his eyes fixed on the floor.

"Sudden? It's prompt and sensible . . . no messing about. *My* mind's made up. The girls are here now . . ."

Blaedud looked up, dazed, shaking his head as if coming out of water. Everything was moving too fast for him.

"Yes, their ship put into the River ten days ago, and it's taken most of that time to fetch you back from the College of Priests. Backwards and forwards I've had to send—Syweddyd is as slow as a snail and Ceredig isn't any better . . ."

Ten days, and nobody said a word to me, thought Blaedud.

"Anyhow, they're here, with their retinue, all prepared for the marriage in another five days—the new moon, of course—and then another moon for the feasting, and the ship will sail again, taking the *other* princess home, which-ever she is. So you see, it's all planned out."

Yes, thought Blaedud, it's all planned out.

The servants completed his adornment, a wide gold torque round his neck, gold buckled sandals, bracelets on his arms, and the small gold diadem that marked him as the High Prince. They went out from one thatched building to another, to the great hall, a building like a barn, its lowest courses built of stone. Inside, the hall was lit by the fire that burned under the smoke-hole and by torches round the walls. It was full of people, King Hudibras's followers, and a group of strangers, the Ikkeni and their two prin-cesses, with nobles and ladies and servants in attendance. The strangers were in their best robes, brightly coloured and obviously costly and besprinkled with jewels of gold and bronze. But the two princesses stood out the brightest of all.

One was dark and wore a robe of bright green, a colour Blaedud had never seen in a cloth before. Her hair hung down in luxuriant black curls, shining and springy, she had big bold dark eyes and carried herself proudly with a swing and a dash. The other, in gleaming white . . . Blaedud's heart missed a beat. Where had he seen her before? That smooth golden head, so neatly shaped, those eyes, dark and soft like a dove's—yes, a dove's. That was it—the white dove on the nest, who was also a girl . . . He stepped forward, impulsive, and put out his hands to her.

Old Hudibras stopped him with a frown. "One moment, my son. Your Honour—" this to a grave bearded personage standing behind the princesses—"you must excuse him. It seems he's over-eager . . ."

A laugh ran round the company, and Blaedud crimsoned.

"Let all be done properly," said the King. "Let the herald announce."

A pompous old man in bronze armour stepped forward, blew a trumpet and proclaimed,

"My lord Lud-Hudibras, son of Lud, son of Brutus Greenshield, welcomes to his domain and castle of Caer Troia the noble lord Kincar, brother of King Coel-Cangu of the Ikkeni. The noble lord Blaedud, the High Prince, son of Lud-Hudibras, welcomes King Coel-Cangu's daughters, the Lady Guendollen, the elder, and the Lady Elen, the younger." And each made obeisance in turn, the dark sister first and then the fair sister.

"And this," said Hudibras in his loudest voice, "King Coel-Cangu's elder daughter, is the bride of my son Blaedud—" and he led forward the dark girl. "What's her name?" he added in an anxious aside. "Elen—Guendollen—which is it?"

"Guendollen, my lord," prompted Kincar, the uncle.

"Guendollen, then, bride of my son Prince Blaedud. Take her hand, my boy."

For his very life Blaedud could not keep back the cry that rose to his lips.

"No—no—not that one! The other! *This* one . . ." and dashing aside the clasped hands of his father and the dark princess, he seized the hand of the golden-haired Elen, while all the assembly gasped and murmured and growled.

Hudibras wheeled about and grasped Blaedud by the shoulder and shook him as he would have an impertinent page.

"What, you dare! You—you—you—" His face purpled and the veins stood out on his forehead. He struggled for speech. Kincar stood frowning and clenching his fists. The men of his escort laid their hands on their daggers. Hudibras, meeting Kincar's hostile look, recollected himself, cooled his rage, and dropped his hand from Blaedud's shoulder.

"My lord Kincar," he said in a choked voice, "I beg your pardon for this affront. My son is a child and a churl and shall be whipped as such."

Blaedud seemed to come out of the spellbound daze that held him. He drew back from his angry father's reach and looked from him to Kincar, coldly and steadily.

"I am no longer a child," he said, so that the whole hall heard him, "nor do I wish to be thought a churl. Father, it will not serve your honour to have me whipped. But I do indeed ask your pardon, and that of the Lord Kincar, and most of all of these ladies. But I spoke out of the impulse of my heart, as a Druid speaks when the spirit is on him,

28

and my words were not altogether my own. I meant no discourtesy, but the spirit does not choose its words. My noble father, honoured Lord Kincar, honoured princesses, I hold by the words the spirit made me speak. I will take the Princess Elen for my wife, though she is the younger, and no other at all."

There were angry murmurs throughout the assembly, especially among the Ikkeni, Hudibras and Kincar, now united aginst Blaedud, muttering together, the two princesses drawing apart and eyeing each other doubtfully, the dark one pale, the fair one blushing and then pale again.

"Has anyone thought of asking the ladies themselves?" said Blaedud. He searched the faces of the two princesses anxiously, but could not read the play of expressions that passed over them. His father loomed above him like a thundercloud, a thundercloud from which the inevitable bolt must fall. In all the hall he could not see one helpful face. Yes, one! There at the back, just come in, was his friend and tutor the Druid Ceredig. A quick sympathy flashed between them. In the years past they had often read each other's thoughts, and over the years of his boyhood Blaedud had come to know Ceredig as an unfailing friend. In one glance of the eye, he sent out his plea for help.

There was a stir at the back of the hall. The voice of Ceredig was heard.

"In the Name of the Gods, let me pass—a vision, a vision, a vision . . ."

His white head, with the head-veil dishevelled, struggled through the crowd.

"What is it?" Hudibras snapped, exasperated.

"Oh, royal Lud-Hudibras!" shouted the Druid, his voice rising upwards to a shriek. "A vision, a vision, a vision—oh, let me speak!"

Hudibras shrugged and turned to Kincar.

"We must hear the messages of the Gods. It would be unlucky not to. Say on, honoured and ancient Ceredig."

Ceredig stood rolling his eyes and panting.

"Oh my Lord, I saw it as I looked on the stars. The line of your noble forebears—I saw first Brutus, and then Locrine, and then Locrine's queen Guendollen, and the queen Guendollen's hands were stained with blood, the blood of the innocent Sabrina. Guendollen brought death to her husband Locrine, and bloodshed to all the land of Brutus—let not the name of Guendollen be the name of a queen in Britain, not the name of Guendollen!" He twitched and contorted his face, and seemed to be foaming at the mouth. Hudibras could not help but listen, his eyes fixed on the seer's convulsed face.

"I hear, O revered Druid," he said in a hushed voice. "What then? What do the Gods say?"

"The Gods say," the Druid enunciated with difficulty, as if his mouth were half paralysed, "The Gods say—and mark this, O King—the Gods say Elen, the mild moon, she who is full of light, Elen is the bringer of good . . ." He groaned and fell to the ground. They carried him out of the hall.

Hudibras turned back to Kincar, subdued, with all the fight gone out of him.

"My lord—you see? We cannot fight the Gods. What say you? Will your royal brother let our son take the younger daughter instead of the elder?"

Kincar looked bewildered and troubled.

"Why, sooner than risk bad luck . . ."

They all seemed to have forgotten Blaedud. Kincar turned to the princesses.

"Well now, the ladies should have some say in the matter, should they not?"

"Why, yes," agreed Hudibras. "I suppose they should."

"What say you, then?" Kincar turned to the girls. "Lady Guendollen—can you agree to be set aside?"

"It's all one to me," said Guendollen sullenly. "I had no choice before and I've no choice now."

"And you, Lady Elen?"

She stepped forward, her eyes uplifted and full of light.

"Oh, yes, yes!" she said softly, and put her hand in Blaedud's.

"And so, I suppose, that settles it," said Kincar, with a reluctant smile.

"Yes, I suppose that settles it," agreed Hudibras. "Well, Blaedud, you're lucky. Or your Ceredig's a clever fellow, which is it? Oh, but we mustn't speak against the Gods, must we?"

Bird that Flies Not

So Blaedud and Elen were married, and were in great bliss and delight. He found in her all he had hoped for and more, and she gave her heart and body to him with all the singleness of her nature. It was the perfect "happy ever after" marriage. The Princess Guendollen was not at all ill-contented. During the feasting that went on, five days' waiting for the new moon and the wedding day, and one full month after, she found no lack of company. She could have had a dozen lovers, but she took none of them. She would wait till she got home, and secure a more important prince. Hudibras and Kincar got uproariously drunk together. Rud and Dardan were full of benevolence towards Blaedud and shyly admired his pretty bride, but kept at a little distance. Perhaps, they thought, if they waited he would come back to them. But Blaedud and Elen wandered singing in the sunshine by day and slept in the paradise of each other's arms by night.

It was the eighth morning after their marriage, and the early sun was filtering through the chinks of the wooden lattice that covered their window. Blaedud woke and looked with quiet pleasure at Elen lying beside him.

Their bed was a great box-like structure, with straw below, and on it piles upon piles of sheeps' fleeces that one could sink into, with costly fur rugs on top. This bed had sheets too, of coarsely woven whitish linen, a luxury few could afford. They slept naked between the sheets, as everyone did, sheets or not, and saw no reason to do otherwise.

"Are you awake, my love?" he said.

She gave a sleepy murmur and opened her eyes.

"Now that we are truly one, I can tell you my great dream."

"Oh," she said, opening her eyes a little wider, "I had a dream, a lovely dream. We were walking, you and I, over fields and fields of beautiful flowers. It was lovely. What was your dream?"

"I don't mean that kind of dream," he said. "I mean—a dream all my life. A thing I mean to do, a thing I'm always wishing for. A thing I was born for. Elen, my love, it will be wonderful. I'm going to conquer the air."

She looked at him, frowning, and rubbed her eyes.

"Conquer the *air*?"

"Yes—men have conquered the sea by means of ships. If the sea, why not the air? Elen, I am going to find out how to fly. I shall fly like a bird."

He was glowing with the wonder of his imagination, trying to convey it to her. But at the word she drew back in fright, and he felt her whole body grow tense.

"To fly? Oh no—oh no, you mustn't. It's terrifying—it's death. I can't bear it."

"But why, my dear? I can do it, I know I can do it. No more dangerous than fighting or hunting."

"Oh, but no. It frightens me. Not flying! You mustn't, Blaedud. I don't like it. I forbid it."

"Darling, how can you forbid it? I tell you, I must."

"And I tell you, you mustn't." She was shrinking back from him against the pillows, cold and shaking. "I know you'll get killed if you do, and I'll be left alone without you—oh, I can't bear it! Promise me you won't do it."

"I promise I won't talk about it any more if it frightens you, my dear."

"Not talking about it isn't enough. You mustn't even *think* about it—you mustn't *do* it. Promise me."

"Dearest, I can't promise."

"Then you don't love me." She turned her head into the pillow and began to cry.

"Oh, don't cry, my dearest. I do love you, you surely know I do. But you don't understand. This is my *geas*."

Everyone in the Tribes of Britain knew about the power of the *geas*—it was a man's destined object, the thing to which his life was directed. It was laid upon him by another, to do this or that or to avoid doing this or that. To succeed in it was enough justification for having lived—to fail in it often meant death.

She turned her head, again with a twitch of suspicion. "Your *geas*? Who bound it on you?"

"Oh, someone—I cannot tell you." Not even to Elen could he tell of the Bird-Woman.

"A woman?"

"Why, yes, a woman—but not as you think . . ."

"A woman? I hate her—and I hate you too . . ."

32

"Oh, my darling, what have I done?" He winced as if she had struck him.

"No, you don't love me, and I don't love you any more . . ."

"Now, sweetheart, enough of this foolishness," and he took her in his arms, overwhelming her like a bear, although she struggled and beat her fists on his chest. He held her firmly until she tired and her fury spent itself in tears. Then he comforted her tenderly and after a while she slept, but the tears still glittered on her eyelashes and he knew that when she woke she would not have forgotten.

He was sore at heart. Of all things he had not expected this, that she, his white bird, should not wish him to fly. She, the only one in his life, for whom he had defied his father and all his tribe, and all her tribe too—and would so again, oh, a thousand times! But she, his bird, she would not let him fly. She would draw him back from his destiny, his *geas*. He had been so sure that she was part of his *geas*. He had seen her, sitting close, smooth, white, on the nest as he hovered above her. And then, with a sick pang, he remembered how the Bird-Woman had dragged him away, shrieking, both of them shrieking—he struggling and shouting as he tried to get down to his white dove, the Bird-Woman yelling above him, "No, no, no! Death, death, death!" Once again he felt the struggle, and sweated and grew hot and cold with anguish, and felt his heart thud and falter with the strain. He looked down at his bride as she lay asleep, so white and golden—his at last, and not his. Or was it that he was hers and not any longer his own? The tears coursed down his cheeks.

"Heart of my heart," he whispered. "Heart of my heart, you will always be. But oh, why must you cut my heart in two?"

I'll See You Soon

Now the moon's feasting was over and the guests from the Ikkeni must return to their home. The whole court, from King Hudibras himself down to the scullions and kitchen-

33

maids, went down to the great river to see the guests on board their ship. They travelled down in a great shapeless crowd, most on foot, some on ponies, for it was no more than a morning's march down to the River, though perhaps longer to get back to the heights. The princes and chieftains rode their stocky moorland ponies, and the princesses did the same, in long thick dresses tucked up round their legs. The two wives of King Hudibras, who were the mothers of Rud and Dardan, being older ladies, were carried in litters. Behind them came rough wagons, jolting over the stones, carrying the possessions of the departing guests and the rich presents they were taking home. Many of these were astonishingly fine jewels, for simple as the clothes and furniture of these people might be their goldsmiths' work was gorgeous. Some of this represented the bride-price of Elen, which Hudibras had magnanimously doubled. And Guendollen carried round her neck a string of rare pearls, of four different colours, white, black, yellow and pink, which extended to her waist and gave her very great satisfaction indeed.

By the side of the great River Tamis quite a settlement had grown up. Downstream was a fishing village, which the royal party passed by rather quickly because it stank. Further upstream, where a small tributary joined the River, was a place where ships could tie up, a sort of small hard, and within sight of this the King had a hall which he used when he visited the River—near the water but not too near because of the tides and the uncontrollable floods. Between the hall and the ships there had grown up a huddle of small dwellings, with booths and storehouses, some of them lying along foot-trodden tracks, the beginnings of streets, short, narrow and winding. Here the merchants brought their wares and here were cookshops and taverns and lodgings of a sort. A drift of smoke from many wood fires lay over all. Beside the hard was the ship that would carry the Ikkeni up the coast to their town and fort of Coel—later called Colchester—named after Coel, their Sun-God, whose name their kings all bore.

A ragged crowd of fishermen and hangers-on raised a shout of welcome as the royal party went by. Inside the hall a farewell feast was prepared, which lasted well on into the afternoon, with speeches and songs and all the right things said. Afterwards there was more personal leave-taking.

Blaedud bowed low over the hand of Guendollen, now his sister-in-law, or fair-sister. He murmured words of leave-taking.

"A word with you, fair-brother," she said, and drew him away from the rest into a corner.

"I bid you farewell, and happiness," she said, holding his hand. "We shall not meet again—but remember only this. I would have helped you with your dream of flying."

He gasped and stared.

"You would . . ."

"Yes. My sister has told me. She is full of fears and would keep your feet on the ground—but I, I know you can do it. But all that is behind us now, and too late. Fare you well, and forever!"

Suddenly she caught his face between her hands and kissed him. Then, equally suddenly, she was gone. Her attendants gathered round her and bore her away. Blaedud was left staring stupidly, his mind in turmoil.

The departing guests had been seen aboard the ship—Kincar and Hudibras, nicely drunk, weeping on each other's shoulders, Hudibras being firmly led ashore by his chief officers. Guendollen, having wept a little, gracefully, with Elen, had gone below. And at last the cumbersome tub of a ship had been rowed out by the oarsmen and headed downstream, whence at the river's mouth she would turn north along the coast till she came to Coel's City. The ship slowly disappeared round the bend of the river. The home party, in the mellow summer afternoon, prepared for the long drag to New Troy.

Elen was on her pony, disposing her white mantle around her for riding, and a servant held Blaedud's pony for him.

"I think, my dear," he said, "I'll follow you later. A long slow walk—I—I have things on my mind. Let me walk a little. I'll be home by sundown."

"Do so, love," she replied. Her voice was as loving, her smile as sweet as ever—yet he was uneasy.

"Good walking, my dear," she said, "and I'll see you soon."

He watched the cavalcade out of sight.

Other Wings

It took a great deal of walking to and fro along the margin of the river to sort out his thoughts. The sun, upstream of the river, drew down lower and rested on red clouds. Here and there a torch or a fire was lit in one or other of the huts by the riverside.

Blaedud became aware of a woman standing quietly behind him. A tall woman in sombre clothes. She had been there for some time.

"A good evening to you, Prince Blaedud," she said.

He looked at her attentively. She was not young, but neither was she old. She was lean and muscular, and looked immensely strong. Her body was bare to the waist except for a dark cloth drawn tight over her breasts, which were hard and firm, more like well-shaped wood than flesh. Her waist was small and lean, like the loins of a greyhound, and below it a dark heavy skirt flounced out over wide strong hips. He could see leathery brown legs and bare feet with toes that gripped the ground. Her hair, black with a few streaks of grey, stood out in a bush round her head, and her face could not be called beautiful nor yet ugly—it was strong, bold, animal. Silver jewellery clashed round her as she turned.

"Prince Blaedud," she said, "listen to me."

"I listen," he said, between curiosity and fear.

"You wish to fly. I can teach you how."

He started back. Astonishment took his breath away.

"You can—what? Who are you?"

"A neighbour of yours, Prince Blaedud. I have always been near you but you have never noticed me—why should you? You may call me Ragan, if that means anything to you. Well—do you understand what I offer?"

"You can teach me to fly?"

"Yes."

He stepped closer to her. She smiled, showing her teeth, which were white and clean. The rest of her was not. He shuddered—and yet . . . ?

"Do you come from Her?" he said.

"Who knows?" She shrugged her muscular shoulders. "I

serve a Goddess. Undoubtedly She sent me—whether you know Her or not."

Huge excitement swept over him.

"And—what payment would you want?"

"I would want payment, but we are not hucksters. We won't talk of it now. When I have shown you, then I will tell you what I want."

"Not—not my soul?"

She laughed. "By the Goddess, no! What do I want with souls? Be content. I'll only ask you for that which you can well spare. Now, will you come with me?"

"I will come," he said.

"Then, quick and quietly, this way."

She seized his wrist in her hard dry hand, and led him. First they went along the darkening river bank, westward, upstream. Long reeds and sedges grew to the water's edge, whispering as the evening breeze got up. Back from the river's edge and among the reeds were huts, poor and squalid. Not much light in any of them. They went on till they came to the last one, and there she led him firmly in.

It was dark, stuffy and ill smelling. A dim fire glimmered and cracks between the withies gave a little light. There was a table, cluttered with vague objects, and a low bed—not much else.

"Oh, I know it's no palace," the woman said, "but come in, king's son—many a poor hut hides the riches of wisdom. Have you found the secret of the Air in King Hudibras's curtained chambers?"

He came in and she closed a wicker hurdle behind him for a door and tied it with a thong. On the table there lay an earthenware vessel with some kind of dark sticky stuff in it. She stirred it with a wooden spoon and it gave off a pungent aromatic smell.

"Now," she said briskly, "doff your clothes, and lie down on this bed."

He hesitated—for one thing the bed looked none too clean. It was covered with thick greasy sheepskins, and in the dim light he could imagine he saw fleas and bugs moving in it.

"Come, make haste," she said. "Oh, no need to be

37

maidenly shy—I'm old enough to be your mother. As for the bed, if it's good enough for me, that can fly, why not good enough for you? Take it as a test of your resolution. So now, lie on your belly, with your back uppermost, so that I can anoint you with the holy ointment on your shoulder blades. That is to make the wings grow."

Tensely he did as she bade him, resting his face on his hands to keep it off that sheepskin. He felt her begin to rub that dark viscid stuff into his shoulders, stooping close above him. Her hands were hard but not rough and, after the first shock of contact, not unpleasant. The rhythmical movements of her hands on his shoulders was soothing and she seemed to be singing a soft monotonous song. The strange smell of the ointment rose to his head like the fumes of wine.

Presently she left massaging his shoulders and went and sat over in the shadows. If he lifted his head off his hands he could see her watching him. She had very strange eyes —the irises were pale, not dark, and shone out with a grey light from her brown face. He began to feel a strange sensation in his shoulder blades, a kind of tingling and swelling, as if they were indeed growing.

"I think my wings begin to grow," he said.

"Then come—no time to lose!" She sprang to her feet and grasped his hand, jerking him up. "Let's be going. Your wings will grow as we run."

She led him, dragged him almost, at a run out of the hut, and whirled him away over the dark river bank. Night had fallen now but the full moon was rising, red among the mists. He could see the wan gleam of the river, the dark banks, the moon, and nothing else. At first the woman led him running—she was surprisingly light footed. The things on his shoulders swelled and grew—then they were wings! He could feel them and sense that they responded to his will like arms or legs. Great strong feathery wings, like a swan's, like an eagle's. He beat the air with them and rose up—his guide rose in front of him, and she had wings too. Effortlessly they both soared up together. A huge exultation possessed him—freedom, and delight and power! Up and up and up—he could feel the air currents below him and leaned into them like a bird. He had no need to learn—

he knew what to do. He was complete and fulfilled at last. He was flying.

Dimly he could make out the ground below him, so far away it hardly mattered. The red moon was still low and by its light he could trace the river, but hardly anything else. The woman Ragan flew always a little ahead of him, leading the way. He thought, of course, of the Bird-Woman. But this was not the Bird-Woman, he was sure of that. The Bird-Woman was all bird, save for her face and her long white arms—this one was all woman save for her great wings, and now she was naked, as he was. There was no attraction about her nakedness—hard and impersonal she was, like an animal. Yet somehow he did not find her as repulsive as before. The rapture of the flight put all else from his mind. That, and a glorious deep breath of pride. Oh yes, the Bird-Woman had always flown above him, ready to clasp him in her hands if he fell. This one flew ahead and beckoned him to follow. He was no longer a child, but a man.

Far away there were voices in the darkness, and then other forms flew towards them—winged humans also, like big dark birds. They cried out on a high exultant note and Ragan answered them, shrilling into the sky. The newcomers took no notice of Blaedud but called back and forth to Ragan in an unknown language. They all began to swoop downwards.

Below them the ground became visible, a wide smooth plain, with here and there a grim lonely stone. The assembly seemed to be converging on the plain.

"Oh, must we land?" he cried to Ragan. "I'd like to go on and on—further and higher . . ."

She gave no answer but led him down with the rest. The company of dark flyers circled low and alighted on the ground in a ring. There was something in the middle but in the dim light he could not see what it was. He alighted on the grass without difficulty, no frantic tumble, an easy touchdown like a heron.

Now they began to dance. Somewhere there was music, pipes and tabors playing a dreamlike compelling tune. The flying people danced lightly and easily, their wings lifting their weight, their feet only just touching the ground.

Blaedud felt that he could do the same. Like cranes, he thought, like cranes he had seen dancing their mating dances in the marshes. They joined hands, and he and Ragan joined with them, and all went round in a great ring, widdershins. Then with one accord they lifted their joined hands and swept inward towards that which was in the centre. He could see it now—one of those awesome solitary stones, and standing on it a woman. He hoped that it might be the Bird-Woman but quickly knew it was not. This was a wingless woman, for she needed no wings, gleaming white and beautifully naked, with horns on her head and strange ornaments about her neck. The newly risen full moon was gone from the sky. She was the moon.

The winged people were now paired off, men and women, whirling round each other, closely clasped. Blaedud, standing still for a moment, observed them—of the women, some were young and some were old, and a few were beautiful. The men—tall strong young men all, and as each one turned his back his long hair fell sleek and smooth—but as each man's face came round again, it was not the face of a man but of an animal. One was a wolf and one a bear, another was a bearded goat, another showed the whiskery muzzle of a seal, another the snout of a hedgehog. Yet from behind they were all young men . . .

Ragan whirled him into the dance, not clasped together but hand in hand, spinning out at arm's length. Their wings lifted them, and the other winged people around them beat the air like a flock of black crows—some couples dropped away into the darkness . . .

The white woman on the stone raised her arms, shaking a kind of rattle with maddening intensity. She stirred up the dance, higher and faster, higher and faster . . . Then far away a cock crew. It sounded through all the noise and the music.

A voice cried, "The dawn, the dawn!"

Like starlings, the crowd was up and away. The white lady was gone, only the old stone remained. Blaedud felt himself swept up and away, round and round till his senses left him.

He woke lying on cold hard ground, Ragan's arms round him, clasping him to her. He tried to rise and thrust her off, but could not.

"Your love, your love!" she was gasping into his face. "Love me, love me, my prince. You must, you must, you *shall* love me!"

Her moist mouth was smeared over his, frantically seeking his kisses. He turned his head away, from side to side, trying to avoid that frightful avid mouth.

She shook him by the shoulders, fastening her claws on his shoulder blades.

"Oh, the love of your body!" she moaned. "Take me, take me! You said you would give me—what I asked. Didn't I make you fly? Now the payment. Your love, your love!"

He thrust her off him, sickened by the smell and touch of her. His head was reeling and aching as if he had been dismally drunk. Evading her clawing hands, he managed to stand up. She remained crouched on the ground, glaring up at him like a cat.

It was dim cold morning and he had no idea where he was. Somewhere desolate and barren and unknown. He was still naked, but she had her dark bedraggled skirt on. Wings? There were no wings.

"I dreamt it," he said.

"You lie!" she spat at him.

"I say it was all a dream, a bad dream."

"You dare to say it! That was no dream. I made you fly —I gave you wings. I took you through the air, I brought you to the Sacred Circle and under the eyes of the Goddess of my people. Deny it if you can!! And now, now I ask you for payment."

"I never promised you that."

"You did, you did. Remember your own words."

His head ached and he could remember nothing that he had said.

"What did I say, then?" He edged backwards, for she was trying to come closer to him.

"I said I would ask you for what you could well spare, and you agreed."

"Then I cannot spare what you ask of me."

"Liar again!" she spat at him. "Liar, and promise-breaker, and false."

"Don't come any nearer me—sorceress!"

She rose to her full height.

"You call me sorceress? You refuse me what I ask—after what I have done for you? Then Blaedud, son of Hudibras, I curse you. Promise-breaker, deceiver, bargain-cheater—I curse you, curse you, curse you." Three times she stabbed her fingers towards him in a forked movement. He could feel the hatred vibrating out of her towards him. Then she lifted her voice in the shrill ululation he had heard when she was flying. It went through his aching head like an arrow.

He broke away from the spot, and ran and ran and ran. Whether she pursued him or not he did not know, he only ran as if the nightmare was after him. He hardly noticed what kind of country he ran through, save dimly he knew that the light increased as the sun rose higher. At last he found a small stream and plunged into it over his head, again and again, trying to wash away the smell of the witch.

At length he climbed back onto the bank, his head clearer. He had no idea where he was and could recognize no landmarks. He was alone and lost in a strange country, completely naked and quite helpless. Home—he had to get home. He had let all the tribe go without him, and somehow he must get back. But how, but where? At the very thought he felt sick and faint again. Why had he ever left them? Elen, his lovely wife—oh, he must get back. But he could never tell her . . .

Grounded

The sun was warm now and he dried himself, and then he noticed that his shoulder blades were burning. Where the witch had rubbed that ointment, where those illusory wings had seemed to sprout, where the woman's hands had clawed him—he put his hand over his back and felt the spot. It was sore and tender and the touch of his hand pained him.

42

Two patches the size of hands on his back. He suddenly noticed what he was doing—leaning against a tree, he had been rubbing his back against it. Scratching his back on a tree like a beast—he, a man and a prince! With a shock of shame, he checked himself. But his back went on itching and burning. He bathed again in the stream, pouring the water over and over his back, and still it burned. Then he dropped his head on his knees and wept. So this was the hag's curse. Her poisoned ointments, her devilish wings. One of those terrible ills that gnawed the skin and decayed the flesh. Leprosy—he had heard of leprosy.

After a long time, he roused himself and looked about him. He was sick and miserable, not hungry but thirsty, and he drank again from the stream. The sun was now past the noon and the day began to cloud—where could he go for the night? Perhaps some hut could be found, where the folk would take him in in return for one of his gold rings . . . He looked at his arms and hands. No rings. Not a trace of the rich array of gold rings that used to be there, on upper arm, on forearm and on fingers, the insignia of a chief's son. Of course, the witch had taken them all. Now not only did he not have a rag to cover himself with, but not a particle of gold to buy help or to prove his title. Nothing in the world—naked as he was born, but not, not clean and whole as he was born. Those horrible sores on his back . . . A leper. Accursed and unclean. He could never go home now, even if he knew the way. And he wept again, and the flies buzzed about his shoulders.

With stumbling steps he followed the course of the stream. Men lived by streams, he thought dimly, for his thoughts began to be dull and clouded with his suffering. Men lived by streams, but wolves came down to drink by streams too. Oh well, let the wolves take him then. He was beyond caring.

At length he smelt woodsmoke. Yes, there were men of a sort. The little low-lying huts of the Brown People, the dwarfish folk that were there before the Men of Troy. Dark dirty little huts of dark dirty little men. There they were, four or five low black beehive thatches, half sunk into the mud. Pigs rambled all over the ground around them, and the whole place stank.

A Brown Man, a wizened little specimen, came out of a hut and barred Blaedud's path with a spear. Behind him two dogs barked angrily. Blaedud spread out his hands beseechingly.

"Help me," he said, hoping that the man understood his language. "I am a prince."

The man drew his ugly features into a scowl.

"Prince?" he said. "No prince. Bad man. Go."

Blaedud dropped on his knees before the man and, in doing so, the sores on his back came into sight. The man recoiled.

"Bad, bad!" he cried. "Go, go."

"Oh, I beseech you—" cried Blaedud. "By the Gods, by the Father and the Mother—by the Mother . . . !" and he made a sign he had learnt from the Druids, a very old sign, older than the worship of the Druids' Gods. The Brown Man checked and looked thoughtful.

"Come," he said, and led Blaedud to a hut rather removed from the rest and if anything dirtier and damper. The pigs were all round it and seemed to have chosen it for their favoured spot. The man caught up a coarse piece of sacking and tossed it to Blaedud.

"There," he said, "house for you. Now you mind my pigs. All you good for." He laughed, as if something funny had occurred to him. "You mind my pigs. Scratch your back, same like pigs. Perhaps pigs make you better."

He Will Return

Rud and Dardan refused to believe that Blaedud was dead.

"Not old Blaedud," they said. "He couldn't be. Not a chap like Blaedud—not just like that."

"If there'd been a war, he could have been killed in battle," said Dardan. "But we'd have known."

"Yes, we'd have known somehow," agreed Rud. "But there's no war, and I don't think any of the old tribes could be dangerous."

44

"He could have walked into a trap and got robbed and killed, in those huts along the river front."

"Not he—he's too wary. You'd never catch old Blaedud that way."

"Do you think he could have tried the Wings—without us?"

"Why, no. Didn't we make a pact that none of us would, without all three?"

So they argued to reassure themselves, for indeed there were many things that could have befallen Blaedud.

They asked Elen if she knew where he was, but she turned her head away and said, "My lord is where he chooses to be. Do not ask me."

For she was convinced he had gone away with Guendollen. Bitterly she reproached herself for having told Guendollen about his unlucky craze for flying. Of course, she reflected, Guendollen would know how to pretend to be interested, to share his mad notions, whether she cared a straw for them or not—she would encourage him just to win him. By now he must be well away in Coel's City. Why had he insisted that he loved her and not her sister, and then slipped away like that? Oh, he was weak, and a scheming woman could turn him as she wished. But why hadn't Guendollen taken him in the first place and spared poor Elen all the heartache?

So Elen turned to Rud and Dardan with a wan smile. "Forgive me," she said, and then broke from them weeping and ran into her own house and barred the door.

In the first few days, of course everyone thought he had gone with the ship to Coel's City. Why he should have done so, without telling anyone, was a puzzle—except to Elen, who said nothing. But after ten days much consultation was held about sending a messenger to Coel-Cangu for news of the prince. How to send was a serious problem. By sea would be the quickest, though from Lud's Port to Coel's City was a long voyage—but Hudibras had no ship available. The port held only those ships that came from without. Overland was a long and difficult way—first the river and its swamps to cross, then wide forests; or you might go further north till you struck the high ridgeway they called the Ikkeni Track. By either route it might take

45

weeks. Eventually they sent off a party of three messengers on ponies by way of the Ikkeni Track, having ascertained from the Druids the most propitious day. Each had the King's message learnt by heart.

Every day Elen would go up to the timber tower where the watchman had his station, and look out over the river and the land. Sometimes Rud and Dardan were there too, but she would not say much to them. At last, after a whole moon had gone by, there was a sail on the river. The watchman raised a loud shout to the men-at-arms below, who hurried to the King. Rud and Dardan hastened down, and Elen followed more slowly, trembling, and sat for a long time in her own house, waiting. Then she went up to the tower again because she could not bear to wait, and looked over the greenness and mist below. Soon she could make out the small company plodding up the long slope, on foot. There were the three men who had been sent out, and another. They went into a fold of the hills and the dead ground hid them. There was nothing for her to do but go indoors and wait again.

When she heard the crowd around the Great Hall, she ran along the covered pathways and quickly into the hall, entering at the end where the dais stood. The messengers were coming in at the opposite end, and with the light behind them she could not at first see faces clearly. The three came in, and then the fourth. As he came where she could see, she cried out. It was not Blaedud, but her brother.

Hudibras was by her, and put his arm around her. "Father King," she said, "what does this mean?"

He echoed her words thunderously across the hall.

"What does this mean? Why have you not brought the Prince Blaedud?"

The messengers shuffled unhappily forward, and knelt. The young Kerin, Elen's brother, knelt behind them.

"You. Speak." Hudibras pointed with the butt of his spear at the first messenger.

"My lord King—thus says King Coel-Cangu. The Prince Blaedud is not with him. He was not on the ship. By the Sun and by the Moon, by the Father and by the Mother, the King Coel-Cangu knows nothing of him. In token of this he has sent his son the Prince Kerin."

Hudibras stood with his face growing redder, his eyes bulging more angrily. His right arm tightened round Elen, but he never noticed how she grew suddenly cold and struggled for breath. He raised his left arm, clutching and unclutching his fingers, held his breath like a child preparing to howl and, after a second of terrifying silence, let out a yell that shook the roof.

"Wha-a-a—"

Then becoming more articulate,

"War on Coel-Cangu! War on the traitor, the liar, the man-stealer! War on all the Ikkeni! Hear me—I'll not leave one of the accursed Ikkeni alive, man or woman, child or suckling . . ."

He tossed his red-gold hair, and the vibrations of his rage beat back from the walls.

The young Kerin pushed his way to the front, and laid his hand on the angry King's knee.

"My lord King—I swear it, on my life—we know nothing of where Prince Blaedud is. No one of us has laid a hand on him, nor seen him. Search our whole territory, indeed we have searched and not found him. I swear on my father's name, he was not on the ship . . ."

Hudibras hurled the young man back with a thrust of his big foot.

"Guards there—put this man in prison. Let him be tortured every day till he reveals the truth. And you, my men, prepare for war . . ."

He suddenly perceived that Elen, clinging to his arm, had sunk down upon the ground behind him. For a moment his rage was checked. Ceredig, in his white robes, stepped quietly up and took Elen from him.

"My lord King, don't be a fool," said Ceredig very softly.

"Eh? What do you mean?"

"With respect, what I said, my lord King. Why should Coel-Cangu do any such thing? The Prince Blaedud isn't with him, and that's how it is—why should he lie to you?"

"But if he's slain my son . . ." Hudibras growled.

"Now, in all reason, would he have any call to do that? What would he gain, seeing his daughter here," and Ceredig gathered Elen into his arms, where she lay unconscious, "is the Prince's wife? And if, my lord King—*if* she should have conceived a grandchild for you, what are you doing torturing her brother and making war on her father? Keep your temper, my lord King."

"Oh, well—". The big man sighed and relaxed. "You're so often right, Ceredig. Poor girl—let her be looked after. Yes, let Prince Kerin go, and treat him with honour. Well, then, Ceredig—do you think the boy's dead, then?"

Ceredig spoke very gravely.

"I have no vision there, my lord King. But the land is wide and full of hazards. It may well be."

Hudibras turned his back towards the assembly and addressed them without looking at them.

"Hear me. No, we'll not make war on Coel-Cangu. I believe my son is dead, and we will all mourn together."

And with that he sat down and covered his head with his robe, and every man in the hall did the same. From the back of the hall the women raised the keening, and outside the sound was taken up, thin and eerie, and spread to the bounds of the fort, and echoed over the ramparts. But Ceredig, his grey face full of compassion, carried Elen away and gave her into the hands of her women.

Man Among the Pigs

"I can't believe it," said Rud to Dardan. "Not old Blaedud —not just like that. Why, one of us would have known, somehow—we always did know. Remember the time he fell from the Wings and we couldn't find him, but you had a feel, just a feel, of exactly where he was?"

"I remember," said Dardan. "But this time I've had no feel about him. But I'm sure I would have known if he were dead. Anyhow, we must go and look for him."

At daybreak the next morning, in the hut which they shared, Dardan woke Rud.

"Listen, Rud. I've had a dream about old Blaedud. I knew I would. We've got to go and look for him."

Rud sat up, suddenly wide awake.

"Yes—you'd a dream? Go on, what sort of dream? Where was he? How was he?"

"I don't know anything," said Dardan. "Only that we must go and look for him, now. I didn't see him—nothing." He gave an embarrassed laugh. "All I saw was pigs. Nothing but pigs."

They told no one, for they feared that Hudibras might interfere with their search. They instinctively felt that the blundering old man might have forbidden them to search. So they slipped away, simply leaving a message with their servants that they were gone hunting.

Long and weary indeed was their hunt. Summer ran into winter, and still they sought. It was hard to make a systematic search, for so much of the country was unknown, and there were no maps and not much means of measurement. But for a start they followed the river, going upstream.

There came a day in early spring when they came upon the tracks of a large herd of pigs.

"Look," said Dardan, "pigs, and not wild pigs either—too many together. They've eaten all the winter acorns and are moving on in search of more. Wild pigs don't do that. These are farmer's pigs. Remember my dream?"

"Surely—but what would pigs have to do with Blaedud?"

They followed the track all that day and rested near the track by night. The next morning they took up the trail again, and at last came in sight of the herd. There was a man with them, huddled under a piece of sacking.

"Oh, it's not him," said Rud, and turned away disappointed.

"Wait," said Dardan, "he may know something," and he went towards the wretched creature.

"You!" he called from a distance. "You, swineherd—"

The man lifted his head, and looked, then suddenly half rose, though still crouched and stooping. He stared stupidly, and then began to run towards them.

"What on earth—" began Rud.

The man drew nearer—his hair hung over his face, so dirty that one could not guess its color, his face was encrusted with grime and sunk into a maze of despondent wrinkles. It was a face no one could recognize, but the eyes shone fiercely out. He struggled to speak, as if long unused to speaking.

"Dardan," he said. "Rud."

With a cry of joy they ran forward and Rud, regardless of the filthy rags, laid a hand on his shoulder, crying, "Blaedud, found at last!"—but Blaedud shrieked in pain and flung away from his touch.

"You mustn't touch me," he panted. "Look—" and he threw the rag off him and turned his back towards them.

They stood appalled, sickened. It was worst on his shoulder blades, but it had spread all over his body. The sight was a terrible one.

Rud spoke very gently. "How did it happen, brother? Come, you must sit down and tell us. Tell us everything."

They sat under a tree, and Blaedud carefully sat five paces away from them. When Rud had produced the horn of wine he carried and given him a drink, he told his story, with many hesitations and falterings.

"And so," he said, "I cannot go back. I must remain dead."

"Oh, no, no!" they both insisted.

"We daren't go back without you," said Rud.

"Why—" with a touch of his old quick brain asserting itself, "did you tell anyone you were searching for me?"

"Why, no, we didn't—"

"Then there can be no blame to you. Let me be accounted as dead. For I *am* dead."

"You're not!" Dardan insisted stoutly.

"And what about the Lady Elen?" said Rud. Blaedud shook as with an ague and a tear trickled down his grimy face.

"Most of all I can't go back to her. Don't you see? I'm defiled, unclean, ruined."

"There are physicians—"

"I don't believe any physician can heal me. Once I met a solitary Druid among the rocks of the wilderness. I besought him to heal me, and he could not. He gave me salves but they only made it worse. He told me I might pass it on to others. He said it was some kind of leprosy."

"Leprosy!" At the terrifying word they shrank back.

"We'll kill that witch if we ever find her," swore Dardan.

"That would do no good. Don't add curse to curse. Nothing can help me now. My dear brothers, for the Gods' sake go away and let me die."

"We'll do no such thing."

"At least tell nobody that you've seen me."

Dardan and Rud exchanged glances. They were both thinking that it would, indeed, be hard to tell Hudibras, still harder the Princess Elen.

"At least we'll do this," said Rud. "Here, in this pack, are clean garments, a pair of sandals, some wine and some food, and also some gold rings and pieces. If ever you should recover—and the power of the Gods is great—these will help you to get home. Follow the high ridge, and then get down to the long river. Follow that, and sooner or later you will come to Lud's Port."

They stayed till the next day, making camp near the herd of pigs. Blaedud let them kill a pig and roast it over a fire and, in spite of all his protests, they fetched water from a spring and carefully washed him and clothed him in one of the two clean garments they had brought. They packed the other clean garment away with the gold and the sandals. Next morning, reluctantly, they left him and went on their way together, unable to find a word to say to each other.

The Pigs Know Something

After they had gone, Blaedud sat a long time in thought. Then, stumbling over the acorn-covered ground, he made his way to the rough shelter of boughs that he had made for his temporary sleeping-place, and, wrapping up the spare garment, the gold and the sandals carefully in a hide of leather, he buried the bundle under stones below the floor of his hut. Perhaps some day—who knows? They *said* the Gods were good . . .

He had his regular routine by now. Each new moon— for even the little dark men could measure time by the moon—he would round up his herd and take them back to the encampment. The little dark man who owned the pigs would look them over—he could not count, but he would know whether they were more or less than last time —and he would give Blaedud a supply of hard bread, made of barley meal mixed with ground acorns and baked into round pancakes with a hole in the middle through which they were threaded with gut. Possibly he would also be given a scrap of honeycomb, and always a skin bottle of heather ale. This was one of the few good things the little dark people had, and Blaedud found it comforting. He would go away to the hut they had allotted to him and get drunk for a couple of days. This was his wages and his holiday. Then he would set out with his pigs again till the next new moon, moving in a segment of a circle round the encampment, about two days' journey being the radius. That way they harvested the floor of the forests, area by area in turn, moving on as each patch was eaten up—acorns and beech mast and chestnuts—avoiding elm and ash and pine, for there were no nuts there, though the pigs would sometimes grub up strange roots and fungi from the depths of the soil. He had come to know the pigs by now and to be interested in them. There were some with whom he felt a bitter sympathy, for they too had sores and scabs. Sometimes they gashed themselves on sharp branches or on thorns, sometimes they fought, sometimes insects stung them. Then they would rub the sore places against trees and make them worse. Some of them were in a bad way, and to look at them increased his own feverish misery. "Don't do that, you poor devil," he would say to a hog desperately scratching itself against a tree, "it will only make it worse," and then he would have to struggle to keep himself from doing the same. Sometimes the remembrance of what he used to be and to have rose up in his mind—he, the King's son, the High Prince Blaedud, in the great hall, where there were clean clothes and a fair bed and oh, dear Gods, his lovely Elen—and then he would beat his hands against the ground and groan. At other times he would forget he had ever been anything but the swineherd, caring for his flock, identified with their brutish lives, watching them eat their way from beech mast to acorns and grow fat. And sometimes he would not think at all, but just exist, sunk in a dull apathy, not even talking to the pigs.

But now, since Rud and Dardan had found him, torturing hope had sprung up. That night he dreamt about the Bird-Woman again, as he had not done since he met the witch. She was there, but she did not take him into

52

the air with her. She just perched on a bough and looked at him. And yet he thought there was a glimpse of compassion in her face. "Lady," he prayed, "Mother Goddess—whatever name they give you—help me!"

But for answer she only said, "Look to your pigs!" and he woke.

As he woke he wept. "Look to your pigs!" Was that all she could say to him? To bid him mind his own wretched business? No help, no comfort but that? Too weak to control his weeping, he howled aloud to the forest, and then sat dull and numb once more, staring out before him.

And then he noticed something. The pigs were moving. Not in the usual absorbed methodical manner in which they grazed their way through the acorns, but pushing and scrambling all in one direction, nudging each other, impatient, excited, now and then squealing, making haste to go. He had never seen them do this before. They were moving fast too. He caught up his long staff, his scrip and his bottle, tightened his garment round him and followed them. They were all moving determinedly in one direction as if they knew where they wanted to go and nothing would stop them. He followed them over the high ridge, with the rising sun behind them. They hardly paused all day, but kept always westward. And at last, as the afternoon drew on, they came to a strange place. Long before they reached it he was aware of a peculiar unpleasant smell, like rotten eggs. A bad smell meant nothing to him and he gave it no attention. But then, following the herd, he came up over the crest of a hill and saw a sight. Before him, the hills closed in upon a valley shaped like the half of a bowl, and all the bottom of the bowl was filled with boiling mud. It was brown and viscous and moving, like brown porridge, and in the middle it spouted up and a jet of steam rose into the air, while all over the lake of mud large sticky bubbles burst slowly. Over all there hung that smell of rotten eggs. He gasped with disgust and fear. But the pigs had no fear. They quickened their pace and rushed towards the sea of mud. Alarmed, he tried to turn them, but there was no turning them—they thrust him off and pattered on, down the slope, and plunged headlong into the brown slough. Blaedud watched them horrified. Then his horror turned to amazement, for the pigs were wallowing in the hot mud, not going out too far to the boiling centre, but lying at the edge, rolling over and over with every appearance of enjoyment. They grunted and squealed with pleasure, and plunged and turned voluptuously. He went cautiously down the slope to the edge of the mud and watched them.

Presently one of them came out of the mud, shook itself and lay down on the surrounding rocks. It was plastered all over, but the heat dried the mud quickly and it began to flake off. Blaedud observed the pig curiously—he recognized it as one of the scabby ones, in fact one of the worst, a poor tormented diseased creature, with sores all over its head and eyes—but as he watched it now, and the mud fell away, he saw that the scabs and sores were gone. The beast's skin was clean and unblemished, the reddish hair shining clean as if new, the eyes healed. As the mud fell away he saw that the pig was clean and whole in every inch of its skin. His heart gave a leap. He ran from one to another of the beasts as they came up on to the shore and stood waiting while the mud dried off each one. He remembered the worst diseased ones, and looked for them. Every one was whole and clean, like a new-born piglet.

He walked slowly to and fro. It was incredible, yet—perhaps? Slowly, thoughtfully, he took off his garment and hung it on the branch of a tree. Then, choosing a spot where the pigs had not been, he cautiously lowered himself into the mud.

It was warm and comforting, in spite of the smell. He relaxed in it, and a strange feeling of well-being spread through his body and soothed his mind. He moved and rolled and turned, he held his breath and pinched his nose and dipped his head right under for a moment. It nearly smothered him and yet he was glad to feel the mud on his face and in his hair. For a long time he let himself lie half asleep in the shallows. Then when he felt it was time, he came out and laid himself on the stones.

Very soon the mud began to fall away, and he looked down at his legs. There were no sores on them now, no scabs. They were clean and healed. His thighs, his belly, all healed. He reached his hands over his back, to those dreadful patches where the witch's hands had clawed him —as the mud fell away, not a trace of any sore or blemish

54

or break in the skin. He felt himself all over. All, all whole and sound . . . For a moment he could do nothing but weep with relief. Then he sprang to his feet and danced, naked and free, clean and healed and blissful. Along the shore he danced, among the basking pigs, shouting his delight, his thanks to whatever name he might call the kind Goddess. He turned himself this way and that, letting the sun fall upon his newly reclaimed body in sheer joy of possessing it.

"Come, old porker," he exclaimed, slapping the rump of the pig he had first noticed, "you're healed and I'm healed. Now I understand what the Bird-Woman meant—'Look to your pigs!' Of course! Well, may you grow fat on acorns till you're as thick as an oak log! We'll rest now, and at first light I'll take you all back to your master—and then I'll say good-bye to you. I'll have another flock to see to."

The outpost watchman at Troy-Novant, overwhelmed with joy and astonishment, had raced uphill to the citadel. They all came out to meet him. Rud and Dardan at their head. They closed up on each side of him and, arms across shoulders, marched with him into the town. The people laughed and shouted around him. Blaedud held his head high and walked royally, his simple garment swinging round him, a garland of oak leaves round his neck.

"But where is Elen?" he asked them.

"You'll see her," they said, smiling, but would say nothing more.

In the great hall his father stood waiting and caught him up in his great thick arms.

"My son, where have you been?" No reproaches, but only gladness.

"I suffered an illness, father, but now I am well. And, father—I've found a thing that will heal all the ills of men and beasts, I do believe."

"Ha! and will it heal the aches in my old bones?"

"It might even do that . . . But where's my wife?"

"Oh, you shall see her," and he too smiled. "In good time you come. Take him to her," he said, and so they led him away out of the hall to the large hut that was the Princess's house or chamber.

At the door he paused, for she was lying on her bed, pillowed on the sheepskins. His heart missed a beat—what had happened to her? She was pale, but she smiled and held out her arms.

"Oh Blaedud my prince—I knew you would return . . ."

He knelt by her bedside.

"My Elen, my life—but how is it with you? Why are you here?" He made to clasp her.

"Oh, carefully, my love. One has been here before you—"

"Eh, what's that?"

She uncovered the bundle that lay in her arms.

"Look, your son. Ten days ago."

Ten days ago! That was the very day on which the Goddess of the hot springs had healed him.

He gathered them both into his arms in an ecstasy of joy. The Goddess was good indeed.

FLIGHT THE SECOND

I Must Know More

"The Gods be with you, my love," he said, as the ship waited for him.

"The Gods go with you—I lend you to them for a year and a day," she said. "For a year and a day only that you may go, as you wish, to learn wisdom. But no wings, my love, remember!"

"No," he said, "no wings. Unless I need them to fly back to you?"

He kissed her very tenderly, and then his three children waiting behind her—Lir and Bran and little Cordeil. Then he strode along the planks and was aboard the vessel that was to carry him to the World's Middle and the warm sea whence the first Brutus came.

It was seven years and more since he had come back from the Hot Springs. Seven years, and three lovely children. No wings, he had said. Well . . .

All those years she had supposed he had forgotten his mad dreams of flying. Little did she know of the long patient experiments he had been making, year in and year out, with Rud and Dardan. And that was not really deceiving her, he told himself, for they had made it part of the Men's Mystery which no woman might ever know. For Blaedud, taking his two brothers with him, had enrolled himself in the Druids' secret school, and had been initiated into the next grade of their mysteries, the grade in which they studied the secrets of nature. As part of their studies, the three young men set themselves to learn all they could of the mystery of flight—how birds flew, and how insects, why the great gulls could glide in long sweeps and never move a wing, while the little finches fluttered their wings all the time and the dragonflies' wings whirled so fast you could not see them and they seemed to stand still in the air. Model after model they made, wings of leather, of linen, of stretched membrane, and—very costly—of silk, but none carried them far. Still they tried, spending weeks sometimes in their secret haunt in the Isle of Foam where they had spent their boyhood. They still kept the cave there, and there they made their experiments. And because it was the Men's Mystery, Blaedud told himself, he was not really deceiving Elen.

We can see them now, the promise of their boyhood fulfilled in their manhood—Blaedud red-headed, massive, thickset, with powerful arms and legs and rather prominent blue eyes, his red hair in a straight fringe across his wide forehead; Rud, lighter coloured, more blond, less heavy in build; and Dardan, always different, long, lean, dark, with a sardonic smile and expressive dark brown eyes. Certainly his mother had been of the Older People.

So, on these expeditions that were said to be the ritual hunts of the Men's Mystery, they betook themselves to their secret workshop. But no matter what they did the secret of flight eluded them.

"We don't know enough," Blaedud often said. "We try this way and that, but it's no good. I think it must be a matter of measure—so much weight against so much thrust. But how to measure it, and *what* to measure? Can man measure the weightless air?"

And even the Druids, who could measure the days and the years and the stars, did not have the answer.

Following the principle of imitating birds in every respect, so that they might perhaps hit upon their secret, the three made themselves suits of feathers. These were laborious to make, since every feather and every tuft of down had to be stitched on separately, on strong woollen cloth. The best needles that could be had, which were of bronze, were not very fine nor very sharp. They drove them in with a pad of thick leather, like a sailmaker's "palm," with infinite labour and pain and grumbling and swearing. There were slaves who could have done the work, but none but themselves could be admitted to the secret; so they sweated and cursed and bent the needles and gashed their fingers.

At last the suits were made and they put them on in the darkness of the cave and stepped out into the light. They took one look at each other and doubled up red faced and gasping with laughter.

"D-don't you d-dare to laugh at me, D-Dardan," spluttered Blaedud.

"I can't help it—you—you—you look such a damn fool—"

"L-look at yourselves, both of you," whooped Rud. "Talk of silly fools—"

"Great fat rooster you look like, Rud," gasped Blaedud, pointing with a shaky finger. "And Dardan, he's like a moulting heron."

"Blaedud, what's he?" retorted Dardan, "oh, he's the owl, the great downy owl, with round eyes—"

They waddled about together like clowns, reeling and helpless with laughter.

"Boys," said Blaedud, striving to compose himself, "if they'll help us to fly, it doesn't matter how damn comic we look. Come on, we've got to try them."

So they did, with their wide wings made of eagles' pinions fixed on reeds. But all that the feather suits accomplished was to cushion their fall a little on to the landing mattress of brushwood and hay which they always kept below their jumping place. Here they plopped down on their backsides like three fledglings in a nest and lay there laughing again. After that they discarded the feather garments, in spite of all the trouble they had cost, and abandoned them in the thorn bushes, where the foxes and rats eventually disposed of them.

Now they had a little luck, or they would have despaired altogether. Taking off from their platform, with one strong sail stretched above his head, with the wind towards him but not too violent, Blaedud floated a few yards and landed gently. In huge delight, they all three tried again. But the wind and the weight and the point of attachment of the sail were never again quite right. They tipped forward or backward, or slid sideways or just dropped, and eventually the sail got broken.

"We don't know enough," Blaedud said again and many times. "We should measure. But how should we measure? Where can we learn?"

So they returned from the Isle of Foam, having ostensibly accomplished their secret rites, and found the court in a bustle. Old Hudibras had made up his mind to make an expedition to Blaedud's hot springs and to try them himself.

The King's Bath

Hudibras the High King set out to try the hot springs with all his court in attendance, his chiefs and his counsellors and especially the Druids. He made the journey groaning and grumbling, in a litter laboriously carried by eight men, constantly changed from a team of twenty-four. With him went Ceredig and Syweddyd, as Chief Druids representing the wisdom of the tribe. Blaedud had carefully marked the way he had taken from the hot springs, along the great line of hills north of the river, and they had no difficulty in finding the place, but the way was rough and long, and the litter-bearers had a hard time of it as well as plenty of abuse from the King.

"By my father's head," said Hudibras as they neared the end of their journey, "this is a fine sweet smelling bower of roses you've brought us to, young Blaedud! What is it— all the eggs laid by Ceridwen the Hen for the past hundred years . . . ?"

They made a camp, well upwind from the sulphurous fumes, and the men-at-arms cut branches and made a hut for Hudibras. Then for the next few days Syweddyd and Ceredig examined the mud, looked it over, tested it in every way they could. They studied the aspects of the stars and made long calculations. They took auspices and haruspices and went over the ground with the holy divining rods. Finding some places where the water came out clear from a height above the mud, they tasted the water, very cautiously. They found it very unpleasant to the taste, but undoubtedly medicinal, and made a note that it must be taken only in judicious doses, else the purifying power of the Goddess could certainly purge a strong man to death.

And meantime Hudibras, much to his annoyance, was carefully prepared by the Druids. When he had ordered them to come with him and make sure that everything was safe and canny, he had hardly expected them to extend such zeal to his own person. Praying he could stand, but fasting . . . ! And drinking that horrible stuff into the bargain . . . !

After three days they solemnly proclaimed that there was no evil in the hot mud but certainly a blessing from the Goddess, and the King might safely try it. So, a spot having been selected where there was no trace of pigs, Hudibras was supported down to the verge by Rud and Dardan, supervised by the two Chief Druids, and cautiously lowered into the mud.

His rheumatic grimaces turned to a pleased grin as he felt the warmth. He lay and wallowed, like a great boar himself, flexing his stiff arms and legs. The Druids counted the time on a knotted string, then, when they judged it was time enough, the two young men hauled him out and helped him to the bank. Here, as he dried off, his house-servants gently brushed the drying mud off him with soft towels. Blaedud watched him intently, as did all the others. Suddenly the King jumped to his feet and let out a roar—but it was a roar of delight.

"I'm fine, I'm fine!" he shouted. "Not an ache, not a pain—joints as supple as a youngster's—look! Come on, you boys, I'll fight the lot of you, race you, anything you like . . . No, perhaps not now," and catching Ceredig's eye he sat down again on the cushions his servants provided. "I think I'm sleepy—lazy—anyhow I'm well. I tell you, Blaedud, your hot mud's a marvel." He waved his arm. "All right, the rest of you—go ahead and try it for yourselves."

The rest of the court, especially any who had aches, pains or sores, quickly followed his example. Within the next few days all the sick people of the tribe, and many from other tribes, made their way there, and quite a number of them were made better. Naturally not all of them, but quite an impressive number. Syweddyd and Ceredig went to and fro with serious professional faces, taking notes in some kind of writing of their own.

"Tell me," Blaedud asked Ceredig, "what is the name of the Goddess of the healing waters?"

"One of her names is Sul, or Ysyllt," he answered.

"How does she appear? What is the sight of her like?"

"We do not know. She is a Goddess."

"But has she wings—does she fly like a bird?"

"Oh, that I cannot tell you, but why not? She has great powers, and is merciful."

"Indeed she is merciful. We must call this place the Waters of Sul."

He walked with Hudibras along the shore of the mud lake, Hudibras enjoying every step he took with his newly liberated joints.

"Tell you what we'll do," said Hudibras, "we'll tidy the place up a bit, make channels for the mud and proper baths where people can lie. We'll lay down stone paths. We'll have conduits from the higher levels, where the water comes out drinkable. And yes—up there we'll have a temple, a temple to your Goddess."

"Oh, yes," Blaedud agreed with enthusiasm, "a fine temple to the Lady Sul herself."

"And another thing," said Hudibras, looking with some distaste towards a part of the lake where a few wild pigs were even now rolling about in the water, "we'll fence it all about and keep those pigs out."

"No, father, no!" Blaedud's tone was vehement. "You can't do that. You mustn't shut the pigs out. It was the pigs that led me here and showed me how to get healing. If it hadn't been for the pigs . . . Oh, no, you mustn't shut them out."

"Lot of stinking porkers—"

"Yes, but don't you see, father—they are under the direction of the Goddess. If you shut them out I'm sure it would be unlucky. I think She might withdraw Her favour—how do you know the springs might not dry up, or go cold, or lose all their power?"

"Oh, well—I suppose so. Wouldn't do to anger the Goddess. Well, bless the pigs—we'll leave a place, like over there where the mud spills out, and let them have that. I hope the Lady Sul will approve."

A Master of Stone

Hudibras sent for cunning workmen from overseas—Rome, or even Greece, it was all one to him—to set the pavements and to raise a noble temple to the Goddess above the springs. There was plenty of money to do this—Syweddyd and Ceredig saw to that, making sure that the pilgrims that flocked to the place for healing paid their proper dues. The workmen came from Gaul, though they originally came from much further away, and they laid flat pavements of stone, and cleverly constructed channels for the water and the hot mud to flow, and baths large and small where people could lie in the mud or in the water, as the Druids directed. And behind the pools, where the hills closed round in a cup shape, surrounding the holy springs, a temple rose of squared stone such as no man in those parts had yet seen. The men of Troy-Novant could pile up walls, stone by stone, expertly fitting the smaller stones among the larger to make strong and solid dry-stone walls—Cyclops style, the foreign workmen called it—and they could even plaster them together with lime, but they could not do more. Here and there at certain holy places there stood huge single stones, the work of men long before Brutus, and some men who had wandered far along downs and ridgeways had a rumour of a vast circular Temple of the Sun and of Time, which could only have been raised by enchantment. But this, the new Temple of Sul, was different. Stones were hewn out of the nearby quarries with iron tools such as the Trinovantes did not have—measured exactly, so that one stone would fit upon another and hold together without lime. The pattern was simple, though not like any the Trinovantes had seen before—a plain flat-fronted porch with pillars on which the cross-lintels rested direct. Behind was a little cell for the Goddess to inhabit and on each side of the cell a conduit where the clearest of the water gushed out. All the simple shape was worked over with carvings, symbols of men and beasts and Gods.

Blaedud was very interested in these workmen. There were five of them, a master, two men and two youths. All appeared to be free men, not slaves, and wore the red bag-shaped caps that signified freedom. They wore thick leather aprons, whitened with the dust of the stones, and protected their hands with rough leather mittens. They were swarthy skinned but not black, their eyes were brown and lively, their hair rippled. The older men had bristling beards and the Master's was crisped with grey. Blaedud stood and watched them as they worked.

The Master was adorning the wall behind the porch with carved symbols, cutting them into the stone with hammer and chisel. Blaedud knew many of the signs he had carved, such as would be known anywhere—a wavy line for water, the sun, the moon. Everyone knew these. But one the Master was carving now—that was different. First a triangle of equal sides, then in the middle of that triangle an eye. Lines going out to the sides, like rays of light.

Blaedud stooped over the carver's shoulder and whispered,

"Master, where do you come from?"

Without looking up or checking the movement of his hand for an instant, the other replied,

"From the East."

"And where are you going?"

"To the West . . ."

Then Blaedud said something else, that made the Master lay down his mallet, slip his chisel carefully into the pocket of his apron, and turn to face the younger man. He stretched out his hand to him and Blaedud clasped it. Then more questions and answers passed between them. The Master smiled broadly.

"Fair enough, young Prince. I'll call you my brother. But you don't know enough yet."

"Oh, good Master!" exclaimed Blaedud. "That's what I tell myself so often. I *don't* know enough, and I wish to know more."

"You've been well taught to start with. Your Druids have the Light and they know something, but not all. Not very much of what *you* want to know. Come to my dwelling when work is done, after sunset. We will talk."

The Name of a Master

Long and earnestly they talked in the close little hut over the small smoky fire. Blaedud told the Master Stoneworker all his aims and desires—he felt he might do this, for the man was already an initiate of the Men's Mystery in some form, and deeper, much deeper, than he was himself or indeed, he suspected, than were Ceredig and Syweddyd.

"Yes, that is where our secrets lie," the Master said, "and we may not reveal them to anyone. Measure, balance, proportion. Without them nothing can be made, nothing that will stand firm or resist the pressure of the elements or use the elements' own powers. That is what we were taught by the Perfect Masters."

"That is what I long to learn," said Blaedud, his eyes glowing. "Can you not teach me?"

"No, my prince, I cannot. We are under vows, all of us, not to teach any part of our science to any who are not initiates of our Degree."

"But I—you recognised me?"

"Only in the first Degree of the Mystery. You have not taken the other steps."

"Then I wish to take those other steps—Master, cannot you initiate me?"

"I am sorry. I cannot do that. Not even if we could call a perfect Lodge together. Only at the right place and by the right Master can you be given the secrets."

"Then who is he, and where must I seek him?"

"The Master of Masters—he whom they call Pythagoras. He dwells sometimes in Massilia, sometimes in Sicily, sometimes in Greece. In all those places he has colleges and visits one and then another. If you would learn those secrets—and my son, I am sure your desire is true and laudable—you must go to the East whence I came."

"How can I go to the East, to those places that seem so far off?" The strange names echoed in his ears, he turned them on his tongue, trying to get the shape of them, but they conjured up no image except that of something infinitely far away, over a long long road, over the sea, over long long roads again . . .

But the Master was speaking. "How? Why, the same way as we got here. On foot, on horseback, over many roads, over the sea in ships, and by roads again. These places are not beyond the world's end. Men come and go there. My home is there," and he sighed. "There the sun shines all the time, except when the brief rains come to bring us plenty. There the olive trees, the palm trees, the pomegranates grow, and the fireflies dance in the long grass by night . . . ay me. There I will go when this work is completed."

"Could you not take me with you?"

The Master drew back and looked at him in the flicker of the fire.

"Willingly, my son, if you were a common man. But you are a prince and have your work to do. Wait, wait awhile, till you can leave your land. Perhaps when your son is seven years old, and you have other sons, that your father be not left without an heir—"

"It is a long time to wait. Oh, good Master, tell me this— why cannot the Master of Masters write a letter telling me his wisdom and send it to me by messenger, if I cannot come to him?"

A look almost of shock came over the Master's face.

"Write the secrets? Oh no—never. That would be the greatest of sins. The secrets must not be written. Why, if they were, anyone might seize them and read them and use them, even foolish men who did not know their value. Even wicked men who would put them to ill use." Blaedud recalled how Ceredig and Syweddyd had said the same thing once long ago.

"No, my son," went on the Master. "They must only be given from mouth to ear and only to those who have prepared their hearts and minds. Oh, I know . . ." and he looked at Blaedud with yearning affection, "I know, my son and brother, that your heart is prepared. But you must wait. No good ever came of moving before the time. The time will come. For the present, learn all that your Druids can teach you, and continue your own trials. The Gods will send help in due time."

So now, after seven years, the call had come. Lir was seven, Bran was five, and the little daughter Cordeil was three. And a ship, larger than most, had sailed up the River Tamis and the captain had put into Blaedud's hand a wax tablet written in Greek letters, which said, "It is time. He is at Massilia. Come." For signature it bore the picture of a radiant Eye surrounded by a triangle.

First he told Rud and Dardan about it. Quite of their own accord, they did a thing that surprised him.

"Yes, of course you must go," said Rud, "and bring back knowledge. No, we can't go with you, for we must take care of things here. Dardan . . ."

He beckoned Dardan to him, and each solemnly took up the attitude of oath-taking of their boyhood—each kissed his finger, wiped it on his knife, and then drew the finger across his throat.

"See it wet, see it dry, cut my throat if I tell a lie."

And then they repeated together, with hands clasped.

"We, Rud and Dardan, sons of King Hudibras, do solemnly swear by the Father and by the Mother that we will guard our brother Blaedud's inheritance while he is away, and that we will not seek to take the kingdom for ourselves. If either of us does that, let the other cut his throat and let the Old Hag of Darkness take his soul. So let it be."

As they loosed hands, Blaedud caught their hands in his.

"Dear brothers, that was not necessary. I know you won't seek the kingdom, and I trust you. Both look after Elen for me."

"We'll do that," they said.

"Only . . ." said Dardan.

"Well, what?"

"Only—we sometimes wish—or *I* sometimes wish . . ."

"You wish what, brother?"

"That you'd go to war instead. There'd be more fun and more profit, and the young warriors get impatient—"

"Oh, Dardan! The sort of thing you *would* think of— but I tell you it's no good. Never mind, I'll only be away for a year and a day, and when I come back I'll know secrets that will make you all invincible in war. We'll go to war then, the year after next. Will that do for you?"

So they had to be content with that.

Next he had to ask leave of Hudibras. The old king was ageing rather rapidly—fatter than ever, and soft, his hair growing grey and scanty, his face purplish, his eyes too full. Useless for Syweddyd and Ceredig to tell him he ought to eat and drink less and avoid losing his temper.

"Well, well, my boy," he said creakingly, "I suppose you'll have to go, if it's to get wisdom. A year and a day, you say—well, not a day more, mind that. Going to the East, you say—that stonecutter man, wasn't it, who seemed like some sort of Druid? Syweddyd and Ceredig didn't think much of him, I fancy—but there, I don't think he thought much of them either. Well, there's always something new to be learnt—like the hot springs. Wish I could go with you, in a way, but I'm too old. Hark you now—" and he drew Blaedud to him and spoke low. "It could happen that I was called away before you return—"

"Ah, no, father! Never say it!"

"My boy, it must happen some day, and we all know that we live again and meet again in the Land beyond the Shadows. No matter for that—what I have in mind is that young Lir is your heir and your wife must be regent for him. You boys—" and he beckoned to Rud and Dardan, who had stepped back against the wall. "Come over here. You'll look after the Princess Elen, won't you? And don't let anyone else try to marry her. There are those who would seize the kingdom, don't you see—"

They assured him of the oath they had taken.

Much harder it was to get Elen's leave to go.

She bit her lip, her face reddened with the effort to keep back the tears.

"You must go to seek wisdom, you say. Oh, but my love, why, why?"

"It would be all the same, my dear," he told her, "if I were going out to war. It would be worse, for then I should be going into danger of death, whereas I am not going into any danger."

"There are always dangers, by sea and in the wilderness and among strange men. Supposing—supposing—oh, Blaedud, you're not hankering after that flying, are you? Not again? Oh, my love . . ."

"Hush, my dear," he said, laying his finger on his lip and then on hers. "You must not be concerned with what knowledge I go to seek. That is part of the Men's Mystery and I must not tell you any of it."

"The Men's Mystery!" she cried with bitterness. "That's always the excuse. It isn't fair—"

"But, my love," he said gently, "isn't there a Women's Mystery as well, that I mustn't share?"

"The Women's Mystery?" She shuddered. "That's witch-craft. Let us not speak of it. I am not one of those."

"Of course not, love. Now, let's not quarrel. This is a journey I must take, for the sake of becoming a wise ruler. Just for a year and a day—you'll lend me to the Gods for a year and a day?"

With reluctance, yielding to his gentleness and persuasion, at last she let him go—and braced herself, when it came to the parting, to shed no tears.

The Malice of the Sea

So now he stepped aboard the ship—it seemed huge to him by comparison with anything he had seen before, though actually he could walk the length of it in twenty strides and cross it in four. There were rowers and also a sail. At the stern was a cabin of sorts, a little covered hutch which seemed to him snug enough. The rowers rowed them down the river, and the cheers of the bystanders followed them; and they went out into the unknown. It was a fine summer morning and all was well. Blaedud was filled with huge excitement. Here he was going out into the great world, into something new, into everything new. The salt of the sea blew up from the estuary, the sun blazed on the blue waters, the gulls, his old friends, wheeled and shrieked. The dancing motion of the ship beneath him was like a fine horse—he swung to it and enjoyed it.

By nightfall it was different. The motion of the ship had become a nightmare. A terrible loathsome sickness, such as he had never known or even imagined, had him in its grip. The ship's captain came to see him where he lay in that wretched little cabin. "It's the sea," he said. "It's nothing—you'll get over it." But that was no comfort. The captain offered him drugs, but it was useless, he could not keep them down. He dragged himself, hand over hand, to the ship's side and leaned over the bulwark, retching and spewing, and would have slipped helplessly into the dark racing water, not caring, but that two strong sailors dragged him back.

"Now, none of that, boy—prince, I mean. You come back in here. It's only the sea—you'll get over it."

The other sailor laughed. "Prince or slave, they all get it. But they get over it—most of them."

That was no comfort at all. Then, as he lay exhausted, a dark numbness came over his brain, and he looked up and there was the Bird-Woman.

"Come," she said, "I'll take you out of this. Look into my eyes."

He looked—they were deep brown, so deep brown as to be almost black. He floated up to her, feeling no more sickness, she clasped him as she had done in his childhood, and in a moment they were up and flying clear of the ship. He could see it below them, wallowing in the storm, but he was free of it and out of that hell of waters. Up and up, and here the air was calm and the moon shone down on a fleecy floor of clouds, and he could not see the sea any more.

"Spread your wings and float," said the Bird-Woman. And strangely, he found he could spread his wings. He glided below her, under her shadow. He could see the great winged shadow that she cast, thrown on the floor of clouds below them. His own shadow was swallowed up in it.

"We have left the sea," he heard her saying. "No more storms for you. Here we go, high above the forests of Gaul. No long roads, no wild men or beasts. We shall cross the mountains, high, high up. You will see their frozen tips."

"Oh," he cried, "how much better to travel this way! Why don't men always—?"

He heard her laughing gently. "Not yet, my boy, not yet. That is what you have to try to do. Here I am carrying you in the wind of my pinions because I love you—I can't carry all the world. Perhaps some day you will teach men how to fly—when you yourself have found out how to fly without me."

How long they drifted together through the skies he could not tell. There may have been many days and nights —he saw the day come up in splendour across the fields of cloud, sometimes the clouds parted below them and he could see rivers and woods, plains and hills, and once, a surpassing wonder, white peaks of snow piercing the clouds. The colours of sunrise displayed themselves, and then the blue and white of full daylight, and rainbows, full circles instead of the arches seen on earth. They flew through the middle of a circular rainbow and sometimes their shadow moved below them in the centre of another rainbow. The sunset colours surrounded them and suddenly night came again. It may have happened many times.

And at last she said, "There is nothing to fear now. You are almost at your journey's end," and she flew down low and laid him gently on his bed—and he opened his eyes and there he was, on a ship that rocked him no more than a cradle, with a blue and smiling sea around him.

One of the sailors lifted his head and gave him a drink. "Well, poor brother, you've slept well enough! Five days, no less. We'd have thought you were dead, but you breathed all right. Maybe that stuff the captain gave, you kept it down better than you thought. All right, up you come then. You'll be weak, mind you, so hold on to me . . ."

But he did not feel weak. He was empty but not weak at all, only ferociously hungry. He looked round the calm ocean with delight. This was a bluer sea than he had ever seen, and odours of Paradise came from the shore as they neared it.

The great bay of Massilia, dotted with islands, lay round them, and there were ships, hundreds of ships, such as Blaedud had never seen before—small ones, but narrow, not like coracles, gliding gracefully under one three-cornered sail, and big ones—oh, huge ships, surely the largest in all the world, the largest there could ever be. He

73

held his breath at their vastness. Rows of oarsmen, ten or twelve a side at least, with their gleaming bronze shields hung all along beside them, and some with another row of oars beneath those. Towering square sails of many colours —some ships had two sails or even more. And when they moved, those great ships, they tore up the water like sea monsters.

On Blaedud's ship the sails had been lowered, and it slowed down. The sailors threw out an anchor, a heavy three-cornered lump of stone, and then they took him ashore in a coracle. No other ship seemed to have a coracle, and the strange sailors seemed to be looking at them curiously and laughed when the rower found it difficult to get the round sides of the coracle alongside the square stones of the jetty. It wasn't like running the coracle on to the muddy shallows at home. Blaedud wondered what those narrow knife-shaped boats would do in a British river. It was difficult, though, to get out of the coracle and on to the hard with any kind of dignity. Two strong longshoremen hauled him up and over, and then held out their hands for money.

So he stepped for the first time on a foreign soil.

To Find the Philosophers

This was indeed different. Round the sea front was a cluster of thatched huts that at first seemed much the same as those along the Tamis. But there were differences. The people were all out of doors—and why not, when the sun was so bright and the sea was so blue? They stood in their doorways or sauntered up and down the alleys. Many of the huts had things displayed for sale—pottery, bright red and yellow, with pictures in black, necklaces of coloured shells, mats and cloths of fantastic colours. Stalls offered wine and cooked fish and pies. He was ravenously hungry and prepared to buy something to eat, but the ship's captain, who had accompanied him so far, said, "Don't waste your money here, sir. This is coarse stuff, only fit for galley slaves. Come further up the town and I'll find you something better."

The stalls did indeed improve as they went up the slope from the sea. The people fascinated Blaedud—they were all so lively and bustling and noisy and laughing. Women as well as men, they all met you with broad smiles, flashing eyes and gleaming teeth in sunburnt faces. All kinds of complexions too, yellow-haired like his own people, red, sallow with dark hair, swarthy, deep brown like old wood or almost black with tightly curling hair like black wool. Many kinds of men he had never seen before, and in such variety of clothes too, scarlet and saffron, blue and purple, pale green, flame colour, white. People with light floating garments that the warm breezes caused to flutter, lovely girls garlanded with flowers—some people, he noted with surprise, both men and women, hardly clothed at all. For the hot sun beat down and Blaedud, in the warm woollen clothing he had worn for the voyage, began to feel stifled in the heat. Three pretty girls passed him, wearing hardly anything but long scarves of the finest linen swathed about them and garlands of roses. They looked him up and down, and giggled.

"Don't stare at them," the captain muttered, "or they'll be after you for money." But it was the girls who were staring at Blaedud. Wide as was the variety of dress in cosmopolitan Massilia, Blaedud was conspicuous. His long plaid, gathered thickly around his waist for warmth, the end flung over his shoulder, was of wool woven into chequers, tan and brown, green and black, scarlet and white, all in criss-cross squares, but more remarkable to the crowd were the baggy trousers, not cross-gartered but hanging straight to his feet, thick and bulky, girt up with a gilded belt a span wide. His red hair and beard and his flamboyant red moustache, as well as his blue eyes set off by his sanguine colour, completed a picture not often seen in Massilia. No wonder the girls stared and the children pointed.

The captain led him into a tavern of a kind quite new to him, not a smoky hut but simply an enclosure of wattles, like a sheep pen, roofed over with vines. A few trees supported the vines and their twirling branches were woven in and out of the more solid boughs of the trees, while the ripening clusters hung overhead. The cooking went on out of doors, and the roofed part was the store where the wine jars were kept. Under the captain's direction Blaedud had an excellent meal of roast lamb, strangely flavoured with mint, fennel and rosemary. "You'd better eat hearty now," said the captain, "if you're going to join the philosophers. They live on just about nothing up there."

In spite of this discouragement, Blaedud took his leave of the captain and went on up the slope of the hill to the higher part of the town. Here he was even more astonished, for there were houses built of stone, not just dry-stone walls up to three or four feet and then wattle and daub, such as he knew in Britain, but built out of slabs of stone, cut and dressed and set neatly into place. The roofs were flat and he could see people here and there sitting on them. Before each house was its porch, with pillars, some just rough pieces of stone, some shaped with art. The men, and sometimes the women, sat on cushions or chairs in these porches and, looking past them, where here and there a door stood open, he could see pictures painted on the walls, such pictures as he had never seen before—tiny men and women and children, and beasts and monsters and garlands of flowers, houses and ships at sea, and rocks with the wild animals leaping over them. He would have stood gaping in the doorways but that fierce-looking slaves stood there and made threatening noises at him, and he thought it best to move on quickly. But the next house was just as rich looking to his eyes, and the next and the next. Flowers grew on the porches in earthen tubs, flowers of kinds he had never seen before, filling the air with scent, and vines clambered over the roofs and spilled down in green curtains over the doors. If this was where the philosophers lived, he thought, their life must be an easy one. But no, surely not here, for through the doors he could see fat men in richly coloured clothes, and pretty girls, and children, and it was as well that he was no longer hungry, for the cooking smells were enticing.

He stopped a boy who from his dress seemed to be a slave, who was sauntering by, whistling, and asked him where the philosophers lived. Blaedud could now speak

Greek reasonably well for a foreigner, having studied assiduously under Ceredig, and with the help of an old Greek slave-man. But his Greek was old fashioned and awkward and the boy grinned at it.

"Oh, those!" he replied. "Good Gods! You want those? Oh well—no accounting for foreigners. Keep on going up the hill, straight as you go, and where there's no shade at all and it's as hot as the Rich God's place, you'll find them —if you really want them."

Blaedud thanked him and gave him a gold coin.

"By Heracles, thank you, sir!" exclaimed the boy. "But don't you go throwing your money about like that—you don't know the value of it, as I can see, and there's a lot of bad people about. Look—one of the big silver ones will do for me. Put the gold one away and don't let people see it. Heracles, what fools there are . . ."

He passed on, whistling again, and Blaedud continued on up the hill. The flowers in the porches grew fewer, and ceased; then the houses ceased, and even the palm and acacia trees. Then there was little but dry rocks and everywhere the monotonous shrilling of some creature that might be a bird or might be a grasshopper—only there was no grass. And the sun grew unbearable and the more Blaedud drew the fold of his plaid over his head for shade, the hotter he became. Then the flies began to plague him. He stood still, worried and vexed and disappointed, and looked back, down the slope, over the town, out to the sea beyond, which he felt he ought never to have left, and wondered what he was doing there, in that grilling wilderness, and how long it would take him to get back to the coolness of the sea. And then a voice spoke out of the rock behind him.

"Seven more steps," it said.

He wheeled about and, without counting seven steps, was round the side of the rock. There was a cool recess and there, quietly squatting on the ground, was the philosopher.

He must be a philosopher, for no one else would be up there. His hair and beard were long and his body sunburnt like old leather, and all he wore was a white linen breechcloth. But he was clean all over, his hair and beard snowy white, his cloth of well-washed linen, his limbs smooth and glowing like an athlete's. His face was wrinkled as with extreme old age, but his eyes were bright and his teeth were sound.

"You are a stranger and seeking wisdom," he stated positively, without getting up.

"That's true," replied Blaedud in his old-fashioned Greek, "but how would you know?"

The philosopher smiled, a very likeable smile.

"Your speech shows you a stranger."

"But—I hadn't spoken—"

"I know. It doesn't matter. And who else would come up here in the heat of the sun? Well now—where do you come from?"

Blaedud was going to say, "From the North," but remembering something he said, "From the East, and going to the West."

"Give me your hand," said the philosopher. "Oh yes, we have been expecting you."

"Pythagoras—" said Blaedud, taking the man's hand as he had taken the Master Stoneworker's. "I seek Pythagoras. Is he here?"

"Ah, no. Two days ago he left us to go to Crotona in Italy. But he told us you were coming and bade us be prepared for you."

"He told you I was coming? But how did he know?" The philosopher smiled and made no reply. "Did he tell you my name, then?"

"He had a name for you. He called you Aithro-batés—he who walks upon the upper air."

The Brotherhood

There were five philosophers—Blaedud's first acquaintance, Menippus; another about the same age but much taller and thinner; a younger one, about Blaedud's own age, not yet five-and-twenty; and two very old ones. The oldest ones were hardly as pleasant to look at as Menippus, as one of them was quite bald as well as beardless, and the other was toothless and partially blind—but then, they were said to be incredibly old and awesomely wise. They still talked cheerfully and gave Blaedud a hearty welcome. Their dwelling was a large cave, where here and there walls had been built, and partitions of wattle hurdles and curtains of leather had been placed. Outside the cave was a circle of flat stones for sitting on and, in the middle of the circle, three more flat stones on which the youngest philosopher laid a plank for a table, and covered it with a white cloth and set out their simple meal. Everything was scrupulously clean.

Blaedud felt more comfortable when they had taken his heavy woollen clothes from him and given him a linen loincloth like their own. They made him wrap himself in a flowing piece of linen, though they themselves sat naked in the sun in front of the cave. "Not at first," they said. "The sun will be too strong for you."

He laughed. "I've been in the sun enough at home."

"Oh, but you don't know . . ."

And it was true—already his face and arms were peeling. They gave him olive oil to smooth on them.

The meal was frugal, yet there were things in it that he could not have found at home. The main part was barley bread and a soup of lentils and onions, which the youngest one cooked and served, but they also had lettuces and olives, which were novelties to Blaedud, and radishes and raw onions and herbs he had not met before. The young man, whose name was Philo, brought in a basket of fruit, apricots and loquats and figs, which he shared with Blaedud. The others looked at the fruit, smiled and thanked Philo, but passed it back.

"These things distract the mind," said the tall thin man, Andreiades. "We may have them if we wish but after a time we wish for them no longer."

They drank nothing but water, which they fetched from a spring ten minutes' walk away. Blaedud had been comforting his long dry walk with hopes of ale or wine and felt a little disappointed, but it was beautiful water, very clear and cool, and quenched his thirst very well.

His first acquaintance, Menippus, laughed as he filled Blaedud's cup. "All you strangers expect wine," he said, "but we have only water, which is the best of all. The whole world lives on water. Neither do we eat flesh or fish. We do not eat anything that lives. So we keep both our consciences and our bodies pure."

Blaedud was thinking that this kind of thing would suit very well in the blazing heat, but what about the winter? He said,

"You say I must be prepared before I meet Pythagoras—how long will that be?"

Menippus answered for the rest.

"We do not know, for each man travels at a different speed. Six months to start with. Then perhaps That Man will appear among us and give you the first initiation or perhaps he will send for you, to Crotona or to Athens or even farther away."

"What kind of knowledge do you chiefly seek?" asked the young Philo.

"Oh—the birds—the birds and how they fly. And how men can learn to fly like birds."

"Ah, then you should talk with the Yellow Man, Klisseos as he calls himself." Philo's eyes twinkled with merriment. "That's Chrysseos as we call him, because his face is the colour of olive oil. He's always playing with flying toys, like a child. But he's very wise and comes from a country a long way off."

"I must find this Klisseos," said Blaedud. "Where is he? Is he one of your brotherhood?"

"He's away in the hills now," said Philo. "Sometimes he wanders away for days, but he'll be back."

So much to do and to see, reflected Blaedud. And he had promised to be home in a year and a day. A year and a day. What could one do in so short a time? But those other places where he might have to seek his teacher—Crotona, Athens, even further—how long was that going to take? Elen—oh, surely Elen would understand.

He was quickly accepted into the brotherhood. He had a corner of the cave to sleep in, with a bundle of straw and two blankets. Before the sunrise, when the cocks first crew, he would be roused by the others, and they all went out in the chill of the morning with earthen jars to the spring to fetch water for washing, for the insistence on cleanliness was strict. Each one had to wash his body all over with cold water and put on a clean loincloth and robe. The young Philo had to wash the two old men inside the cave and Blaedud, as the newest brother, had to help him, a task he didn't much enjoy, but the rule was the rule. Later they had to wash their own clothes and hang them out to dry on the rocks, and the cave had to be swept in every corner, and all the surrounding area too, and all refuse of every kind carefully buried. But first they hailed the Sun at his rising, standing with outstretched arms as the red orb came up over the eastern mountains and intoning the mystical hymns of the brotherhood. A fire would be lit, from which later a flame would be carried to their cooking fire. Incense was placed upon the holy fire, but no victim.

"Do you make no sacrifice to the Sun?" Blaedud asked the philosophers.

"Certainly we make sacrifice."

"But of what? No beast or bird? Not even a dove or a sparrow?"

"No. We sacrifice no blood to Him. The Great Light, of whom the Lord Phoebus is the manifestation, has no delight in blood. He walks through our camp and sees that it is clean. There must be no uncleanness here. When you have been with us longer you will understand."

Having cleansed the camp, therefore, the philosophers would take a simple meal together—as before, mostly rough bread, olives and lettuces. Then, except for those whose turn it was to attend to household matters, they would settle down to the work of the day, instruction and meditation, seated in a ring at the mouth of the cave. The old men would be helped out and seated in places of honour and from them would come the most valuable part of the teaching. So the day would go on.

When the cool of the evening came they might walk together in twos, and naturally Blaedud paired off with Philo. They made a strangely contrasted pair, Blaedud with his thick tawny hair to his broad shoulders, his round red face peeling with the sun, his slightly prominent blue eyes, and Philo the Greek, small, thin and dark, with crispy waving black hair, resilient as steel springs, and his young face already wrinkled round the eyes with laughter.

"I must go soon," said Blaedud. "If Pythagoras is at Crotona I must go there."

"Crotona?" said Philo. "Oh yes. That Man may well be at Crotona . . . But don't go to Crotona. I've heard about it, and I say, don't go to Crotona."

"Why not?"

"Well—I'd a friend who went there once. Let me tell you but don't let Menippus know, or the others. Well, he went there, and you've got to be a man of stone to stand it. First of all you give them, the priests who attend on That Man, everything you possess. Nothing is your own, not even the scrap of cloth you wear. And from the time you start they watch you, and test you, to see if you are controlled enough. Every word, every movement, every gesture—the old priests are watching all the time. They set tests for you —I'd call it setting traps for you. My friend said they would torment him and bait him and tease him to try and make him angry. They told him—my poor friend!—they told him his father and mother were dead, and it wasn't true, just to see if he would cry. Even if you laughed aloud, or laughed at all—"

"But Pythagoras—they say he is good and great. He surely wouldn't treat a man so?"

"Not That Man—you must understand, we call him That Man, we don't speak his name very much. Oh no, That Man is hardly ever there—it's not himself, it's the priests that surround him and rule his college and make the rules. Why, when he comes here, That Man speaks to us as man to man. He's just one of us and I think he's glad to be. But at Crotona . . . The pupils never see him. When he is there he lives behind a curtain. When they think you worthy, and you have passed all the tests, they let you see him for a few minutes. Then you are accepted as a Pythagorean, and *then* the really hard part begins."

Philo paused and drew a deep breath.

"From that day on, for five years, you must not speak another word—not one word, for five years. Think of it!"

"I do," said Blaedud with a sympathetic shudder.

"My poor friend—after three weeks of it he broke down, he nearly went mad. So he asked them to let him go."

"And did they?"

"Oh yes, and they gave him all his money and treasures back, and more besides, and sent him on his way. But after that they held a funeral for him just as if he had died. And one day he met one of them in the market place and greeted him—a man he'd shared a cell with—and the man looked blank at him and greeted him as a perfect stranger. And when he said, 'Don't you know me—I'm Ariston of Corinth,' the other man replied, 'Ariston of Corinth? But he died, and we buried him,' and turned away."

They walked on together very thoughtfully.

"No," said Blaedud, "I don't think I'll go to Crotona. But is there no other place where I can meet—That Man?"

"Why, yes, there's Athens, and some speak of Persia and Jerusalem and Egypt, but they are all a long way off. Now—" he laughed, "if you could fly as you dream of doing!"

The Man with the Kite

On one day in every seven, each of the brethren was allowed a day all to himself, when he might take his scrip of bread and a water bottle and go off alone into the wilderness. This was good for all of them. Blaedud found it very enjoyable starting out in the cool of the daybreak, walking in the exhilarating morning, resting in the heat of the sun, walking again in the evening. Beyond the arid heights were valleys full of greenness and there were also turfy walks along the cliffs above the sea. And it was on one of those walks that he made a discovery.

He was walking in the glorious sunshine along a high cliff, with the lucent blue sea on his right and the long downward sope of yellow green to his left, his eyes dreaming over the vast cloudless expanse of sky, when he saw a wonderful sight. Hanging in the mid-heaven was a bird, such a bird as he had never seen before, hovering as if fixed to the one spot. It was larger than an osprey or a golden eagle, but how large it was hard to estimate, up there in the sky. It was yellow and vermilion and light green and touched with gold. Its wings were motionless but at their tips were little ailerons that fluttered and palpitated.

It had a spreading fan-shaped tail that fluttered also and besides that it had another tail, long, whip-like, that swirled out behind it and cut curves in the sky, and scintillated as it moved. Sometimes the great bird wheeled and veered away, describing a great arc, but its pinions never moved, only the little feathery tips quivered, and always it came back to the same spot. He had sometimes seen a hawk hover above its prey, wings beating and then still and then beating again. He had seen the great seagulls soar without moving their wings, but never any kind of bird that hovered without moving its wings. Its radiant colours flashed against the blue sky. It was the most glorious sight he had ever seen.

As he gazed a voice spoke behind him, a most peculiar voice, high pitched, staccato, like wood striking hollow wood.

"Dear brother," it said, "mind where you are walking."

And it was as well he minded, for he was right on the edge of the cliff and walking blindly out towards the drop. Hastily he stepped back and saw behind him an odd little man, dressed in neatly cut trousers and coat of straw-coloured silk, the coat flung wide open to the waist. The man's face and body were of about the same colour—indeed, the colour of olive oil. His height would not take him much above Blaedud's shoulder, perhaps even his elbow. His hair was very straight and black but streaked with grey, his yellow face was closely wrinkled all over, and there was something peculiar about the shape of his eyes. Long thin moustaches drooped down over the corners of his mouth and mingled with his straggling beard. In one hand he delicately fingered a very fine cord which seemed to stretch from his hand tautly out over the sea towards the glittering bird. The yellow man gave the cord a twitch and the bird seemed to move, swerve, change direction—undoubtedly it was held on the end of that delicate string. Blaedud gasped.

"What marvel is this? What is this bird that you hold on a silken string? I never saw anything like it."

The yellow man laughed, a little high-pitched sibilant laugh that made hardly any noise.

"That? Oh, that is no bird. That is my toy, my plaything. It is nothing—in my country the children play with them. But it is a pretty thing and a charming amusement and harmless."

"What, the children play with such things? Not a bird, you say? But what, *what* is it then?"

"Oh, you shall see. I will bring it down for you."

He began to reel in the string, coiling it neatly on a shuttle. The colourful "bird" circled, lost height, swooped down, and in a few minutes was lying on the turf before Blaedud's astonished gaze.

It was a beautiful piece of work. About three feet long, with outspread wings, it was shaped like a bird, made of oiled paper stretched upon the lightest and strongest cane and all adorned with ribbons and spangles and tinsel. The head and staring eyes of the bird were indicated in bright painting and so were the overlapping feathers. The long tail, with a knot of tinsel on each joint, lay coiled beside it. Blaedud gazed at it and softly and timidly touched it.

"Whence did it come, this miracle?"

"Oh no, brother, no miracle, no, no, no. Not a miracle at all. I made it myself."

"You *made* it? Oh, but you are an artist, a wonder-worker—"

"Not so. Come, it is only a toy. I will show you how we play with it."

"You—would show *me*?"

"Why, yes. But not now. The sun will decline soon and the wind has changed. It is time to put it away." Very carefully he withdrew some of the canes, rolled up the kite with all its pieces into a tube hardly bigger than a fishing rod, and slung it over his shoulder. So they strolled down the hill together.

"Are you he," said Blaedud, "that they call Chrysseos, or Klisseos?"

"Klisseos," the yellow man replied gravely. "They call me the Olive-Oil-Faced Man. At your service," and he bowed quaintly. "But my name in my own home is Chou-lü-tzu." He pronounced the words with a strange up-and-down intonation.

"At your sevice, honoured Chou-lü-tzu," said Blaedud, carefully imitating the other's pronunciation as best he could. "Among the Brotherhood I am called Aithro-batés, the Walker on the Air."

85

"I have heard your name," said the yellow man, again bowing. "That Man told us that you would come. You want to fly like a bird, do you not?"

"Your toy," said Blaedud, breathless, almost choked with emotion, "a big one, a very big one—could one be made big enough to carry a man?"

"Why not?" said little yellow Klisseos.

A Reason for Wine

"Now," said Blaedud, "when I am ready I will say 'Go,' and when I say 'Go' you will push me from behind and you will pull from in front on the ropes. Push and pull as if the Furies were after you. Do you see?"

They had all turned out to see the great attempt except old Eumolpus, who remained in the recesses of the cave but gave orders to Doron, the next oldest, to relate everything to him afterwards. Andreiades and Doron were ready to push behind Blaedud, and Menippus and Philo, below the platform of rock where Blaedud stood, held strong thin ropes attached to the great kite, to pull it forward against the wind. Klisseos squatted on the ground, supervising with a critical eye.

Many weeks had gone into the preparation for this attempt. Plans had been sketched out on sand and with chalk on flat stones. Measurements and calculations had been made by those expert geometers—so much weight, so much surface, so much pressure, here or there the attachments should be fixed to pull in the right direction and distribute the weight rightly. Materials were selected under the guidance of Klisseos, who himself contributed (no one knew from what hiding place) a roll of fine strong silk and a quantity of silken cord. He selected the strongest and lightest canes from those that grew in the cane-brakes below the cliffs. Of these they made the skeleton under his direction and stretched the silk across, securing all with a strong fish-glue that stank horribly. And now at last all was ready. Blaedud positioned himself on the landward side of the great ridge that bordered the sea. He would have the downs at the back of him so that at least a contrary wind would not blow him out to sea. All was ready now, no reason to delay the jump, except his thudding heart. Oh, if only Rud and Dardan had been with him . . . But no use wishing now. He must take the leap. He grasped the machine with both hands from below and—"Go!" he shouted.

They pushed and over he went and the cords tightened from below, tightened and held. As he leapt he could feel the resistance as the kite pressed against the air—he was airborne! Up he went, he soared, the wind upheld him. He heard a shout from below but dared not look down. The rope had whirled itself out of the hands of Philo and Menippus, but he felt no difference. The wind carried him securely, not down but up. He was flying. At last, at last he was flying! He became aware of the air currents, like the currents in a river, and he leant against them as he had seen the gulls do and bear to the right and to the left. And then he became aware of the strain on his arms. He had not expected to be in the air more than a minute or two and now he had been hanging at arm's length for more than ten minutes. Even his iron muscles were giving out. He must get down, or he would let go and drop. But how to get down? Sudden panic gripped him.

Then he heard the Bird-Woman's voice close behind his shoulder.

"Don't be afraid. Keep calm, I'm here. Tilt the great sail forward a little—just a little, not too much. Now you go down."

"I can't hold on much longer."

"Of course you can't. Silly boy, you should have made a bough to perch on, a nest, a cradle."

He moved the edge of the kite forward as she had said and the kite descended, quicker than he liked. He had a moment of terror as the ground rushed up to him, but the innumerable falls he had had since boyhood served him well now. He knew how to fall and landed relaxed, knees bent, rolling over on his shoulder. For a minute he lay dazed.

Then the philosophers were all round him and all over him, laughing, applauding, shouting, clapping him on the shoulders, kissing him on the cheeks. Thinking of it afterwards, he thought that old Doron's garlicky kisses were the worst part of the adventure.

"You did it," they were repeating, "you flew, you flew like a bird."

"Yes, I did it," he said, as in a dream. "I've begun it. It can be done. I shall do it."

They led him up to the cave in a noisy triumphal procession, as if they had been a pack of children, and crowded in to tell old Eumolpus all about it. He sat up in his bed and, grinning all over his chap-fallen old face, reached down into a crevice in the stones behind his bed and brought out a small skin of wine.

"You didn't know I had this, did you?" he chuckled. "Twenty years I've had it there. I thought a day would come when we ought to drink it. We'll drink it now."

So they all drank, even the severe Andreiades, relaxing his leathern jaws into a reluctant smile. Little Klisseos was in the highest glee, hugging himself and nodding his head and singing strange little chants. They all drink to Aithrobatés, the Treader of the Air.

Airy Journey

Now they redoubled their activities, and even the proper work of instruction and meditation was laid aside. For the next was to be the really great attempt, and all the little community took part in the preparations.

The kite was carefully gone over and tested for any strain or damage. Canes, silk, cord, all were carefully seen to. Blaedud could think of some improvements now. For one thing, he rigged a reasonably comfortable seat like a child's swing, made of strong leather, and added a back-sling as a support behind. On this he could sit for a long time and not feel weary. It might be that the wind would carry him a long way this time.

He remembered how cold he had felt up there, even with the Bird-Woman's comforting presence close by him. He seemed to hear her saying, "You silly boy, you should have had thick feathers." So he put on the warm clothes in which he had come from Britain, although they seemed intolerable in the hot sunshine, the woollen tunic, the heavy breeks, and the long plaid which he wound carefully round him so that it would not impede his arms and legs nor leave any loose ends hanging.

And so he stepped out for his second trial. All the company came out this time, even old Eumolpus, leaning on Doron's arm. Klisseos was there before the rest, carefully looking over the kite, running his delicate fingers along the cane struts and the silk cords.

They stood together and prayed to Phoebus while Blaedud prayed in his heart to the Goddess. And Menippus touched the front tip of the kite with oil of spikenard and amber, to consecrate it to the Sun.

Then they all took their stations and Blaedud seated himself on the leathern seat, with his feet firmly touching the ground. He gave the word and ran as they pushed and pulled him—and was off.

Airborne again, confident and glorying. The cords below were cast off, the wind was lifting him, he could feel the warm wind from the valley coming up, and he leaned into it and rose and rose. Up and up in a widening spiral—and suddenly he looked down and cried out in fear, for he had crossed the ridge of the downs and was out over the sea.

Terror seized him—the sea, all that way below him, and he alone and helpless in the immensity of the sky. No dismounting, no descending, no going back. No way but on.

"I am with you," she said very quietly over his right shoulder. "Bend a little to your left. The wind will carry you."

And the wind carried him, on and over. How long, he never knew. It became more like the dream voyages he had made, out of the body, as when he had crossed the stormy Bay and the mountains of Gaul. But this time he knew he was in the body. He learnt as he went, feeling the air pressure, this way and that, turning to it, pushing against it or yielding to it. Sometimes the Bird-Woman spoke quietly to him and told him what to do. Sometimes he knew what to do.

Far off below him he saw land appear, a long rocky coastline caught by the sunshine. Where was the wind taking him? He knew now that he could not get back to Massilia. The wind—or the Gods—wanted him to go on.

The Bird-Woman, close behind him, beat with her great wings and sped him on, faster and faster—no means of knowing how fast, except that nothing he knew of could travel as fast as this, no bird certainly—perhaps an arrow . . .

There were mountains before him. He wondered if he could get to the ground before he crashed into those white teeth. But the Bird-Woman spoke.

"Not down," she said. "Up. Go on."

He did nothing, but the wind carried him up. He left a town behind him far below—could it have been Rome, he wondered? And still on—another sea lay before him now, narrow and full of islands. And then more mountains. Then at last the wind took him downwards. He was over another town now, a town of white houses like Massilia, but with more of them, in its midst a great rocky flat-topped hill, on it a temple and many white images.

The people had seen him coming and were crowded below, all looking and pointing and shouting. The Bird-Woman had gone and he had to get down alone—it was a terrifying moment. Not to crash into that great flat hill, nor into the sea . . . Just in time he spotted a clear plain and, carefully managing the angles of the kite, he slowed down, gradually lost height and, shouting as loudly as he could to the crowd to keep away, he landed, gently pitching forward. Hundreds of the black-haired lively people swarmed round him.

"The Bird-Man, the Bird-Man!" he heard them calling and chattering. Strange names were being shouted—he heard one say "Daidalos" and another "Ikaros," but mostly they cried out "Aithro-batés! Aithro-batés! Treader of the Aether!" and some of them shortened it to the name by which he was known later, Abaris.

The Wise Woman

Old King Hudibras was dying. And Blaedud, his heir, had been away for more than a year and a day.

It was not easy in those days to keep an exact record of time. The Druids did so, watching the sun, moon and stars,

90

and would tell the pople when they had arrived at the long-
est or the shortest day, and when to plant and reap and put
the rams to the ewes. But otherwise it was all rather vague,
day would follow day till the Druids announced that it
was time for a festival. Elen, sitting quietly in her carved
chair by the hearth, made a mark on the doorpost each
day and so counted the time. Soon the year and the day
were gone and she began to hope for Blaedud's return.
Later, she lost hope and just waited, because there was
nothing else to do.

Old Hudibras had grown fatter and redder in the face.
Still in vain for Syweddyd and Ceredig to tell him to eat
less, drink less, avoid losing his temper. There was a feast
in the hall one night when he defied them all and drank
like a giant. At Ceredig's gentle remonstrance he flew into
a rage and roared to the heavens. With all his people standing by open mouthed and no one gainsaying him, he argued
with himself, whipped up his own frenzy, raged at nobody,
at shadows, at his own voice, at the thunderous echoes from
the walls, foamed at the mouth and then suddenly pitched
forward and fell with all his weight across the table, lying
like a log among spilt winecups and scattered meats.
Syweddyd and Ceredig ran to his help and so did Dardan
and Rud, but the King lay insensible, his face the colour
of a ripe plum, his eyes open and staring but with no sense
in them, his breath raucous and puffing as if he snored.
Eight strong men lifted him up and got him to his bed,
where he lay deeply unconscious, not responding to any
of the remedies Syweddyd and Ceredig tried. Then, after
many hours, the purple colour ebbed away and left him
pale, and the labouring breath seemed to cease and he lay
like the dead, but still he was alive.

Elen came and looked at him with pity—he had been
such a fine old man. And a cold fear came over her—what
would become of her now? Blaedud not there and enemies,
she knew too well, only waiting. Little Lir was rising nine
and he should be the next heir, but would he be? And there
were the other children, Bran and little baby Cordeil. How
vulnerable they all were . . .

She dropped the heavy leather curtain over the door of
the King's house and turned away. And then she became
aware of a woman standing waiting for her.

The woman was tall and well shaped, though not young. Her hair seemed to be iron grey but was mostly tucked away under a white headscarf. She had muscular wooden-looking shoulders and breasts, a lean waist and powerful swinging hips. Her face was brown and wrinkled and full of teeth like a wolf's. Many necklaces of silver, with ornaments of coral and amber and bone, dangled from her neck and clashed on her bosom and waist.

"Hail, mistress," she said civilly enough. "I think you need me."

"Who are you?" said Elen, "and why should I need you?"

"My name is Ragan. I have been near you a long time, but you never noticed me—why should you? And as to why you need me—your Druid leeches have tried everything they know on the King, but they cannot wake him from his slumber. But I can wake him."

"You? How do you know you can? How am *I* to know that you can?"

"Let me try, princess!" The unknown woman's voice was full of confidence and reassurance. "Let me try and you shall see."

Elen looked searchingly at her.

"Can I trust you to do him no harm?"

"Why, what reason should I have to do him harm? Is not he our good old King?" A wintery gleam of a smile came and went in her face. "No, but trust me, princess. Let me just stand by his bedside and stretch my hand over him."

"Come then," said Elen.

She led the woman into the great hut where Hudibras lay in his bed. Two women knelt by the bedside, sponging the King's pallid face with herbal juices. Ceredig and Syweddyd looked on from the shadows. The woman Ragan took no notice of them. Standing at the bed's foot, she stretched her hands out, palms downward, over the inert figure of the King and uttered three resounding vibrating words. They echoed against the rafters and the whole hut seemed to shudder.

Then the King moved his head a little, sneezed and opened his eyes.

"Eh?" he said. "What are all these people doing here? Curse of Annwn on you all, you scoundrels! Give me some ale!"

The women and the Druids closed in on him.

"Send all these women away," he said in almost his own voice. Then his eyes fell on Elen.

"Why, it's my little Elen! Worth the lot of them—you'll look after me. Get me some ale, for the Mother's sake."

The woman Ragan, her work done, turned aside with a clash of her necklaces and strode out. Elen ran after her with a bag of money. She took it with the barest thanks.

"My duty," she said. "If he needs me again, your servants know where to find me," and was gone.

A Seed of Doubt

The old King was fully conscious, sat up and recovered his wits and temper, ate and drank what Elen allowed him. But after three days he was seized with fearful pains. He doubled up, his face went the colour of wax and was beaded with sweat, he roared aloud. Presently it passed and he slept but soon it came again. The Druids' potions were useless, even the strong poppy drink that seldom failed.

Elen shuddered as she heard him crying out. "Send for the woman Ragan," she said.

Ragan came, this time in an all-covering dress of white, with a spotless white coif covering all her hair, almost like a Druidess's, and all her jewellery laid aside. Her smile was sweet and reassuring.

Standing by the King's bedside, she laid her hand on his head and he stopped howling. Then she passed both hands up and down his body and he relaxed and slept.

"He has no pain now," she said, "but I'd best be near him in case it comes again."

When he woke he was quiet and smiling and full of gratitude to Ragan. He ordered his purse-bearer to give her gold. But next day the pain came once more and once more it was only Ragan who could soothe him. So it went on.

Soon Ragan was the only one, except for Elen and the serving women, allowed by the King's bedside, and when the King slept Elen let the woman sit with her on the rugs on the floor of Elen's own hut and talk to her.

"Lady," she said, "your lord has been long away. He should be here."

"He'll return soon, I know," said Elen, sighing. "He said a year and a day, but time passes so quickly for men."

"No doubt, lady, when they have other things to do. Your lord is a man of wisdom, a great scholar—ah! What a king he'll make—"

"Please the Gods, but not yet," said Elen.

"Lady, do not deceive yourself. I can relieve my lord King of pain, perhaps give him a little longer to live, but I know, and you know, that his thread is spun."

And it was about this time that one Brogar, Prince of the tribe whose territory lay between the Trinovantes and the Ikkeni, arrived with a retinue of four-and-twenty men to ask after Hudibras's health, to pay his respects and to dine at his table. He also could call himself one of Hudibras's sons, for he said that his mother had been a concubine of Hudibras, though Hudibras had denied him. Elen could well have done without him and his retinue, with the King lying sick, but, as hospitality demanded, she rose to the occasion and did her best to welcome the stranger. He was a tall thin man in his forties, very pale. His face was long and white and strewn with freckles, his hair straw yellow and scanty. His long jaw was a little undershot so that his teeth gleamed out wolfishly and his lower eyelids drooped a little, showing a line of red. Dardan and Rud did not like him and in fact Dardan called him "a white crow, waiting to pick out the Old Man's eyes before he is dead." But Elen rebuked Dardan severely for his discourtesy and shut him out of her good graces for a long time.

Dardan and Rud kept attentive watch over Elen, as Blaedud had asked them, but they also had to watch over the King's domains. The frontiers were not well defined and marauding strangers could come in if the borders were not defended. There were thieves and there were wild beasts too, and who knows what sinister things besides. So they were often called away, though they usually tried to arrange that one of them stayed with Elen if possible. They both had wives and families of their own now, so they could not give all their leisure time to Elen, and when they were with her she sometimes found them preoccupied and in low spirits, worrying about the state of the kingdom or tired from a long day's riding. Although she knew she could trust them to the death and loved them for Blaedud's sake, she often felt them to be rather dull company.

But Brogar went out of his way to be amusing and pleasant to her. His conversation was always lively and he was always at hand and always willing, whether to send his servants running to the market to fetch her this and that, or to scour the woods himself to bring her the first primroses or the first wild strawberries, or to sit at her feet and tell her stories. The children made him "Uncle Brogar" and he would take them off her hands and keep them amused. Elen found him a great comfort in those trying days, while the King's pains grew worse each time and only the woman Ragan could relieve them.

Elen and Ragan sat together in Elen's hut—Ragan had now won the position of Elen's trusted friend and confidante.

"How fortunate, my lady," said Ragan, "that you have the Lord Brogar here at this moment."

Elen reddened ever such a little. Her fair skin blushed far too easily.

"I'd rather it were my own lord," she said. "All will be well when he comes back."

"When he comes back! But, lady—the days pass and he does not come. What will you do?"

"I will wait," said Elen.

"Lady," said Ragan, lowering her voice, "I could show him to you as he is now."

"By magic? You have magic? Oh, but of course you have. Show me, show me!"

Ragan drew from her robe a small round black stone, just big enough to lie in the palm of her hand, very polished, gleaming, black as ink. She placed it in Elen's hand and stood over her, softly placing one hand on Elen's head.

"Now look steadily," she said.

Elen fixed her eyes upon the pool of blackness and saw clouds drifting across it. Ragan stood up tall in the shadows behind her, white robed and quiet. With her eyes on the stone Elen could not see the expression on Ragan's face, gazing out over her head. It was well she could not, for it was a look of the most frightful malignancy and hatred.

"I can see something," Elen said, in a hushed voice. "Something—oh, now I see him. Now I see him, but . . ."

In the crystal she saw Blaedud's face plain and recognizable. She caught her breath, as one might on seeing a loved face beyond all hope, and then behind him she saw another face, a woman's. It was pale, dark browed and dark eyed, and very beautiful. A cloud of night-black hair flowed around the face and behind the hair was a spread of wings, great wings like an eagle's. The woman hovered over Blaedud, encircling him, embracing him with her wings.

"Oh no!" cried Elen. "No, no, no!"

"It is so, lady," said Ragan's quiet voice.

"Take your stone," and she thrust it back into Ragan's hand, shuddering. "Oh, not a woman! Not another love! Oh, Blaedud, Blaedud . . ."

She flung away and sat down, wringing her hands, weaving her head from side to side.

"Tell me that it isn't so," she pleaded.

Ragan seated herself on the ground close by her.

"Alas, lady," she said, "it is true. I did not want to tell you, but it seems I must. Lady, there *is* another woman in his life, and she is a woman with wings, who lures him to fly."

"What is she, then, a goddess or a witch?"

"Let me tell you, lady, if you can bear it."

"Tell on. I can bear anything."

"You remember, when he first disappeared, when your sister went home. He walked away by the riverside."

"He said he would soon be home," Elen said, her heart feeling again the chill of an old grief.

"Yes. That night there was a great gathering of witches around those stones, the Old Stones that were put up by the small blue men before the Men of Troy came. I saw him, and I saw *her*, with her great wings. He called to her in the sky and she stooped down to him out of the clouds like a hawk and bore him up into the air. So she carried him as the witches gathered, all flying, until they reached the stones. There I saw him dance with her, in the circle round the stones, and there was Something there that they worshipped—"

"You saw him? How were you there? *Why* were you there? Are you a witch?"

"No, no, lady. I am not one of them. I would not soil myself with such things. But I was there because I have to be there and in many other places, bad and good, to learn my arts of healing. I was there, watching him—with sorrow, my lady, with sorrow. He never left her side, and when the circle broke at last and they all sought the shadows by two and two—he sought the shadows with her."

"And . . . ?"

"Lady, what more is there to say?"

"Did he—did he love her?"

"Alas, lady."

Elen drew her breath with a sob and shut her eyes. "Oh ye Gods!" she said faintly, "and I thought him true . . . Is it so indeed? You swear that it is so? Woman, if you are lying—"

"I am not lying, lady," Ragan replied evenly. "I swear by Those whom I worship that this is the truth."

"Then the Gods forgive you for telling me," said Elen, and burst into tears. Ragan watched her for a few minutes and then stole out of the hut. Elen wept without ceasing.

At last she stood up and swept her tear-wet hair out of her eyes and listlessly went to the door. Dardan and Rud, perhaps they could give her come comfort. The twilight had fallen and the people were going into the great hall for the evening meal. She caught a young boy hastening by.

"My lord Dardan and my lord Rud," she said. "Where are they? Send them to me. I am not coming to the hall tonight, but I must see them."

"Lady," said the boy, "they went off southward soon after noon today. I had a message for you but I could not come to you for you were with my lord the King, and then you were in your bower with the wise-woman. I was to tell you that they were called away south, for there was bad trouble on the coast—evil men and evil beasts. They could not wait!"

"Oh," said Elen bleakly, and turned away. No comfort there.

Then suddenly Brogar was by her side.

"Lady Elen, you look pale," he said. "Are you well? Let me give you my arm as far as the hall."

DESPERATE FLIGHT

Abaris in Athens

The people of Athens, the small lively dark-haired bright-eyed people, went mad with delight over their Aethro-batés, their Aether-treader. Wherever he went, jubilant and wondering crowds surrounded him. A writer of a later age set down this word-of-mouth description of him.

"They relate that Abaris the sage, by Nation a Hyperborean, became a Grecian in speech, and was a Scythian in habit and appearance . . . Abaris came to Athens holding a bow, having a quiver hanging from his shoulders, his body wrapped up in a Chlamys, girt about his loins with a gilded Belt, and wearing Trowsers reaching from his Waste to the Soles of his Feet."

With his reddish beard and flowing hair and his ponderous woollen clothing, he was a great contrast to the neat dark Athenians in their light linen tunics. The "trowsers" were the most remarkable of all. Scythian horse riders, and Amazons, were said to wear them. The "bow and quiver" was undoubtedly a recollection of his dismantled kite, lashed together in two parts, the long struts and shafts forming a thing he could lean on like a bow or a spear, the rest rolled up into something that might well look like a quiver. When he was questioned about those mysterious things, he would say, "It is my magic arrow." Those who had seen his spectacular entry into Athens said that the thing that carried him was shaped like an arrow head— and so the story grew of his miraculous arrow on which he could journey to any part of the world with the speed of the wind and require no food while he travelled.

It was true that he had not eaten or drunk since he left the cliffs of Massilia in his flight, but he had no idea how long the journey had taken. But on arriving in Athens he was certainly prodigiously hungry and did ample justice to the feast the Athenians made for the wonder man. For many days they talked of nothing else—and what talkers they were! They told him of Daidalos, who had made some kind of wings to escape from Crete, though Blaedud could not get any satisfactory description of those wings, except that they were thought to be of feathers stuck together with wax.

"No, no," he said. "It couldn't be done that way. I've tried. For one thing, the heat of the sun would melt the wax."

"It did," said Timoleos, the Greek who was his host. "Unfortunate Ikaros, his young son—the wax melted and down he fell and was drowned. Poor Daidalos, he had no more heart for flying and never put his wings on again. He hung them up in the temple of Apollo."

"Did he?" Blaedud enquired eagerly. "I should like to see them."

"I'm sorry, my lord Abaris—there was a fire in the temple many years ago and the wings, being wax, were consumed. There was nothing left of them."

"A pity," said Blaedud. "But I wouldn't trust wax and feathers myself."

Outside the neat little white square house, an excited crowd loitered.

"My lord Abaris," said Timoleos, "the people want to know when they will see you fly again."

"Not till I leave you, I think," said Blaedud. "And then, I think, I shall have to wait till my Genius tells me to go."

Timoleos nodded. This was quite understood.

"But I am looking for Pythagoras," Blaedud went on. "I think I was brought here to meet him. Where is he?"

"The great Pythagoras? But of course you would want to meet him. He was here—but he left, just ten days ago. They say he has gone to Palestine, to the town called Jerusalem, in the Persian dominions, where they say a great temple is being built, though to what God nobody can tell us."

"Oh!" sighed Blaedud, "I missed him at Massilia and I miss him again here. No matter, I must go where he is. But I must wait till my Genius is ready to take me."

"You could travel by ship, my lord."

"No!" Far too vivid in Blaedud's mind was the horrible voyage through the Bay of Biscay. "I'll not tempt the sea. But when my Genius is pleased to do so, she will take me on my magic arrow."

So he waited in Athens and met and talked with many wise men, and a few wise women. And he became an initiate in the Great Mysteries of Eleusis, for which the Druidic Mysteries had prepared him, and he learnt many strange and powerful secrets. But always he desired to meet Pythagoras.

The Genius on Lycabettos

Mount Lycabettos stands behind Athens higher than the rock on which the great Temple is built—from its height you can look down on the Acropolis and see the beautiful white Temple buildings below you.

Here Blaedud climbed on a beautiful sunny morning in the Grecian autumn. All round him the bees buzzed in the wild thyme and the cypress trees breathed out their sweetness. Far off the sea murmured and the whole town lay spread below, with the Acropolis like the boss of a shield. There was an eagle wheeling above him in the sky—he watched it, as he never failed to watch birds. It came nearer, circled the mount and alighted beside him. It was the Bird-Woman.

First she seemed like a great bird in every respect, feather-clad body, tail, talons and all, except for the woman's face and floating hair. Then she lifted her wings and deployed them as a cormorant does and they swirled round her, making it hard to distinguish the shape of her body. Her breasts were clothed with soft layers of feathers, white and iridescent, but he could not see her arms or guess whether they became wings or claws or neither. Her wing-feathers were huge, all of rainbow colours, and she shook them with a rattle of quills as a peacock does—he felt a strange thrill at the sound. He had never seen her so intimately before.

"Greetings, son," she said, quite casually.

He made no reply, for he simply could not think how to address her.

"Here you are, where I wanted you to be," she said. "But you must go further yet. You must meet Pythagoras. He has gone south and east, to a place called Jerusalem, where a great temple is being built."

"Will you take me there?"

"That will I, when I am ready."

"I don't think I can fly without you."

"You certainly can't—not that far, at any rate. You have begun—you can glide. But without my help you could not go on and on and steer your own course and pierce through the clouds and the storms, as men will some day do."

"Will they indeed? Oh, if only I could find—"

"They will, but not yet. Not unless you can find how to drive your craft with power, a power not yet thought of. Look!—eastward towards the place where the Persians are —there is the great fountain of fire which they call the Chimaera. There dwells the secret, the subtle oil that will burn inwardly and give off power like a man's heart—"

"Oh, tell me, tell me . . ." But she closed her lips and shook her head.

"Will Pythagoras tell me, if I find him?"

"He might, if he thinks you are ready."

"Then let me go, and quickly."

"Not so fast. Wait for the time."

He ran his eyes round the challenging horizon.

"But the time is so long. Already I have been away from home more than a year and a day—oh, far more, two years, surely? I promised Elen—"

The Bird-Woman frowned just a little and shook her quills.

"If you go running back to her, you'll never find the secret," she said.

He sighed. "But perhaps she needs me, perhaps she is in danger."

Again the Woman pressed her lips together, shook her head, bristled her wings.

"Bird-Woman!" he cried, "or whatever name I ought to call you—tell me, who are you? Are you my mother?"

She looked deep into his eyes. "No, I am not your mother. She has long since gone on her way and followed her own path elsewhere, as mortals do. I am not your mother, though I call you my son," and she stretched her wings softly over him.

"Then," he said, with awe in his voice, "you must be a Goddess. Are you the Great Lady, She whom they worship in that temple below us?" and he hid his face.

"No, child, I am not She. Let us say that I am one of Her children, one that came forth from her, as the Many came forth from the One. Say I am one of the lesser Gods. We are children of the Divine, of the Father and the Mother. But we are not as they are, the great ones. They are Three—and Seven—and Ten—and Twelve . . . But we are many. They are as their nature is and have no parts or passions but what belongs to their nature. But we, who are not altogether immortal, are subject to time and change and death, though far, far longer our span is than yours, alas! And we are subject to the passions—for I love you."

She gathered him for a moment against her soft breast feathers, then she released him and put him gently from her.

"I can love, and I can feel jealousy, so do not try me too far, my dear son. Because I love you, I have bestowed on you the gift of flight, that no man of your generation or many generations to come may have. Other men will have it some day, but not yet—oh, not for long ages yet. But I wish it to be yours because I love you. There is one who does not wish you to have that gift."

He drew his breath in sharply. "I know."

"She fears that she will lose you. She fears the danger—oh yes, there's danger, but not as long as I sustain you. Can she bear it, that your life should be in the hands of another woman?"

"You should have compassion on her," he said. "She loves me and you should know how she suffers."

"It's true, I know," she said, and for a moment her pinions drooped and her dark eyes softened. "But you have your work to do and until it is done I will not let you go to her. Look, you must follow Pythagoras east and southward, and go to Jerusalem."

She gathered her wings from around him and closed them in upon herself—for a moment he saw the shape of her clearly defined, like the perfect shape of any eagle—then she launched into the air above him and was suddenly gone.

Enemy

Elen had watched all night by Hudibras's bedside. It was certain now that the old man had not long to live. Through the long hours she had sat in the dark smoky stuffy hut, close by the King's bed, watching his movements and the contractions of pain that passed across his face and the restlessness of his hands—and thinking, thinking. What Ragan had told her gnawed at her heart. She saw again the dark strange pale beauty of the winged woman—goddess or witch or demon? Ragan's soft solicitous voice echoed on inside her hot and aching head. More than once she looked towards the doorway where, just outside the curtain, Brogar sat watching. He was always attentive, kind and considerate to her. Yes, there was a man . . . Oh, but no. Blaedud would return—Blaedud . . . ? And round again went her thoughts over that same arid track, seeking rest and finding none.

She stepped out as Syweddyd and Ceredig entered and signified to her that she might leave the King with them. The cold white streaks of a cloudy autumn morning lit the sky with melancholy. Brogar greeted her as she went by. She gave him a nod and a faint smile and went on along the covered way to her own hut.

At her door Edra, Dardan's wife, who had long been one of her own ladies, was waiting for her with an anxious look. The two younger children were close behind her.

"Lady," said Edra, "I'm worried. It's the young prince Lir. He hasn't been home all night."

"Mother!" The little prince Bran pushed forward. "It isn't fair. Uncle Brogar let him go off hunting yesterday with his man Kel and he wouldn't let me go with him, nor Cordeil either."

Edra drew him to her and softly hushed him.

"It seems, lady, that the Lord Brogar sent him out hunting with the man Kel yesterday afternoon, and he didn't come home. I couldn't tell you, for you were with the King."

"If my lord Brogar knows about him, he should be quite safe," said Elen slowly and hesitantly. "But they should have told me." Then she turned quickly. "Edra—I don't know why but my heart misgives me. Take Bran and Cordeil and go to your own farm, quickly and quietly. Take as many men of the household as you need. Keep to yourself and see no one. My darlings," and she stooped and kissed the children, "go with Edra for now. I'll see you soon. Now go, Edra, and quickly."

Brogar was approaching in the distance. She stood between him and Edra, who slipped away out of sight with the children. As they went, Elen spread out her heavy dark cloak, to fill Brogar's eye and cover Edra's retreat, and then swept down on him.

"My lord Brogar—where is the Prince Lir? They tell me he went with Kel yesterday and he's not returned."

He smiled. "Oh, have no fear, my lady. I told Kel to take him on a long ride and to let him stop the night at my castle on the south road. A house of death is no place for a young boy. He'll be safe enough with Kel. Trust me, my lady."

"Of course, my lord Brogar." He was so comforting, so kind, so—reliable?

It was cold, and there was no fire in Elen's hut. She crept into her bed and lay huddled under the sheepskins. Her small dog lay in her arms, to give her a little warmth. So tired she was that in spite of her fears and griefs she slept.

She woke to find one of her maids shaking her. "Mistress, mistress, wake up. You must go to the King. They say it is the end."

Hudibras was conscious, but only just. He lay propped up on pillows, Ragan supporting his head, the two Druids on his right and left, Brogar close by and a crowd of chiefs gathered at his feet. Brogar made room for Elen as she entered and placed a chair for her.

The old man's face was curiously changed, with his nostrils pinched and his eyelids fluttering. He reached out a hand to Elen.

"I'm going, daughter," he said, in breathless gulps. "No good—I know I'm going. Blaedud is King after me—Blaedud. Where is he?"

"Not here, my lord King," she whispered to him.

"Not here? But he'll come back. I know he'll come back. Elen, love—don't take another man. Promise me?"

"Oh, surely, father—" A tear splashed down on his hand, as she held it clasped in hers. He looked down, feeling the tear, and pressed her hand.

"I know. He's true to you, child, whatever they say. He'll come back. I'm dying, and I know." His head dropped back wearily.

Brogar leant over him. "My lord King—who is the next heir?"

"Young Lir, of course," he said without opening his eyes.

"Then will you not appoint me as Regent till he is of age, and guardian to the Lady Elen?"

The dying man's eyes opened suddenly, he moved his head from side to side, and struggled with his lips.

"No—no—no—" but the breath came faintly.

"You see? You hear?" Brogar looked round at the ring of intent faces, and Elen noticed how many of them were Brogar's own followers. "He assents."

"No!" she cried shrilly. "He *didn't* assent! He said no!"

"Quietly, lady," said Brogar, deeply and softly. "Do not make a disturbance."

"But he said no! I heard him—I saw his lips move."

"Hush, lady, hush. He is going."

The laboured breathing was growing fainter, the eyelids

ceased to flutter. No more movement. The eyes, wide open, glazed over. Syweddyd and Ceredig bent over the old King and closed his eyes, speaking ritual words. The women near the door set up the keening chant.

Elen, her eyes fixed on the dead face, felt Brogar's hand round her arm.

"Come with me, lady," he said, impelling her gently away. "Tell your maids to pack what you need. You are coming with me. I will take care of you."

"No, no!" she exclaimed, pulling back. "Where do you want to take me? I don't want to go with you. Let me go!" She looked round for Ceredig and Syweddyd, but they were busy about the dead man.

"Come," said Brogar, and smiled. His wolfish teeth flashed and it was as if he had drawn a knife. Over his shoulder she saw the woman Ragan and she was smiling too. Elen saw the quick glance that passed between them— complicity, satisfaction at a plan carried out, dark intention—and at once the whole tide of suspicion that had troubled her turned and flowed the other way.

"Let me go," she cried again.

"Now, lady, you are weary and overwrought," said Brogar. "Have no fear. I am going to take care of you, Lady Elen—oh, very great care indeed."

From Sounion

The cheerful chattering Greeks had all left their work and their homes and in a holiday throng had surged away out of Athens, men, women and children, to see the departure of their hero of the moment, Blaedud Aethro-batés the Air-Treader. Sounion was the place and thither they all followed him. Sounion with its vast cliff over the sea was the best spot from which to launch his "magic arrow." They carried him out from Athens in a cart drawn by white oxen and behind him, on another cart, the "arrow," put together, reinforced, repaired, improved. The people wreathed it with garlands of flowers.

The great Temple of Poseidon at Sounion stood, white and noble, looking out over the sea. Away before it were the blue limitless waters, the fantastic shapes of rocks and far-off islands, half dissolved away in the blue, all in their glorious patterns of beauty. The ground was thick with the little purple crane-flowers. And over all the wind, keen, pure and powerful, swept like the Will of the Gods. "What is that island called?" he asked, and they told him "Helen's Isle." His heart suddenly smote him. Elen!

In the great temple, a sacrifice was made to Poseidon and another to Phoebus Apollo and, at Blaedud's own request, a sacrifice to the Lady. And quietly, in a place apart, he arranged an altar of stones and made a bloodless offering of bread and salt, wine and honey, to the Bird-Woman. Earnestly he prayed for her help, for if she did not help him now he knew he could not fly at all. But he had faith in her.

After the sacrifices they feasted on the sacrificial meats and drank wine to his success, and then they brought the great kite to the edge of the cliff. He carefully gauged the force of the wind, feeling it on his face and against his hands. He clothed himself in his thick "Scythian" garments, with those barbarous "Trowsers," and wrapped his plaid tightly round him. Over his shoulder his friends slung a scrip with bread and raisins, and a skin of wine. And so he took his place on the seat of the craft and his helpers pulled on the ropes. The fierce wind almost snatched the ropes from their hands. When he gave the word—and nobody knew how his heart beat—the men below held hard while others pushed the craft forward against the pull of the ropes. Up it went on the rush of the wind, snatching the ropes from the hands of the helpers that held them before he could signal to them to let go—and he was off and up into the blue sky. The crowd raised a cry of wonder as they saw him lifting away over the islands. He grew smaller and vanished from their view. He, up there, dared for a moment to look down and saw the white portico of the temple dwindling to a snowflake. Then he looked up and She was there.

To the Holy Temple

As before, he never knew how long the voyage took. There may have been nights as well as days but he hardly knew, for a kind of dream state came over him, in which he knew that the Bird-Woman carried him, driving the kite forward with her powerful wings and all the while singing to him, chanting, crooning softly, telling him things. Like secrets learnt in a dream they passed too quickly for him to be aware that he knew them, but many of them were things that came back to him long afterwards. He saw little of the sea and the lands below him but dimly knew that he went over islands and coasts, and there were mountains and a great desert and mountains again. And at least he came down, alone and with no crowd to welcome him, in a dry desert place towards sunset. The ground was rocky and in his right mind he would have dreaded falling upon the rocks, but She carried him and set him down gently in the place where She wished him to be.

The sun was dropping to his right, and before him, which he knew must be the south, were the roofs of a town set upon a hill and in the midst a great stone temple catching the last light. He could see the scaffolding in a criss-cross pattern all over it. Sitting down on the rocks, he rested and refreshed himself with the bread and wine he had brought from Athens, and then set about carefully dismantling and packing his kit. Having reduced it to such a compact form as to be once again his "bow and quiver," he set out and walked towards the city and the temple.

All round him people were journeying towards the city. Strange people—he could tell at once that they were not Greeks. Just as chattering and lively, and talking with expansive gestures as they walked, and yet with a solemnity under it, a sadness even—in the midst of laughter they would suddenly break into tears and lamentations. Their faces were different, a distinctive cast of countenance, aquiline, beak nosed, with eyes deeply set and lined. Their robes were long and brushed the ground and many of their robes were black. The men had shawls or mantles over their heads and the women were all veiled—no bare garlanded heads as among the Greeks. And their speech was foreign, though among them he could hear a few that spoke Greek. He addressed himself to one of these, a man past middle age, trudging beside a mule laden with sacks and bundles, his two small sons running in the dust by his side, his wife following on a donkey with the youngest child in her arms.

"Good man," he said, "what is the name of the city before us?"

The man halted and looked at him in some surprise.

"Why, have you dropped out of the moon that you don't know? *The* City, the only City in the world. The blessed Zion, The Holy Mount of God, Jerusalem itself, the blessed Place of Peace . . . Well, what kind of a stranger are you, to be on the road and not know where you're going?"

"I ask your pardon," said Blaedud very humbly. "I'm a stranger from a very far-off country. Thank you for telling me."

"You speak good enough Greek," said the man. "Well, what are you, a Greek or a Persian? You're not an Israelite, for certain."

"No, I'm a . . ."—how to explain to this man?—"I'm a Hyperborean. I come from the land behind the North Wind."

"Behind the North Wind? It must be very cold there. Now, I'm an Armenian and we go everywhere, but I've never met one from those parts. You must tell me—but not now. We must hurry along or we'll not get to the city gates before sundown, and if we don't they'll make us stop outside till morning. I daren't risk that, not with the wife and children. Come on." He urged Blaedud into a quick walk. Blaedud's long legs took up the pace easily.

The Armenian's name was Vartabeid, which meant that he was a physician. He had a broad forehead and large dark eyes, his hair and beard were black as night and so were his bristling eyebrows. His wife was very beautiful.

"If you are a physician," said Blaedud, "you will know the man of wisdom who lives in the temple. You will know Pythagoras."

The Armenian darted a quick look at him. "There are

men of wisdom in that Temple," he said, "but they don't like foreigners. You will have to be careful. I can go into the city and ply my trade as a healer, but they won't let me into their Temple. None but genuine Israelites. Oh yes, I've heard of Pythagoras, but he's a Greek. They wouldn't let him enter there. You should be very careful."

They had reached the gates of the City, where already the watchmen were lighting the lamps. The walls stretched to right and left of them, all propped with scaffolding, cluttered with unbuilt stones and with the detritus of old ruins. Workmen were closing down their work for the night and walking away with their toolbags on their arms, but he noticed how every one of them wore a short sword on his belt and some of them wore metal helmets. Trumpets were calling them from their labours and back to the City as dusk fell.

A sentry stood at the gate, two guards behind him barring the way with crossed spears. He let the Armenian and his family through but stopped Blaedud.

"Declare your name and business."

"I am Blaedud called Abaris, a Hyperborean, and I am looking for Pythagoras."

"Pythagoras?" The sentry drew back and looked him up and down. "There's no one of that name here."

"I seek a Master of Wisdom," said Blaedud.

"Oh, do you, indeed? Then whence come you?"

Blaedud had already said that he was a Hyperborean, therefore from the north, but he answered, "From the east, in search of a Master."

The sentry's look changed. He drew Blaedud aside from the crowd and asked him certain other questions, to which Blaedud gave answers.

Leaving another soldier in charge of the gate, the sentry took Blaedud into a small gatehouse in the thickness of the wall.

"You can go through the City till you come to the Temple," he said. "Answer them as you have answered me and they will let you through. You must ask for the Prince Zerubbabel. He directs the building of the Temple, and it is said that he knows the secret wisdom of the builders.

But the Master of Wisdom—That Man—he's there, but he mustn't be known. Only Zerubbabel knows where he is, and who he is. For you see, the priests call him a heathen. If they knew he was there, they would drive him out with stones. But Zerubbabel knows that they need his wisdom to build the Temple. Some of us—those who answer to those words—know it too, but even we don't know where to find him. Go, and may the God of your fathers go with you, for we know that the Father of the Gods is One."

So Blaedud went on through the deepening darkness, through the rumour and smoke and flickering lamps of the City, till at length the huge shape loomed above him, black and massive, the great doorway of the Temple, with its brazen pillars on each side. A great darkness, a terrible Presence, brooded there above him and he felt himself sinking away into the ground. Then small lights pierced the darkness of the vast hollow porch and a dozen priests, in linen tunics and turbans, confronted him. They looked so small in that vastness that he could not feel afraid of them.

"I seek the Prince Zerubbabel," he said, and added a word that the sentry had taught him, not the word he had spoken to the sentry, but another. They passed him inside.

The inside of the Temple was enormous, echoing and empty. Everywhere was the smell of fresh plaster and of dust, the feet crackled on fragments of broken stone and tile, ladders and ropes and scaffolding showed bewildering shapes in the small shifting lights of the priests' lanterns. In a little room that seemed to be stuck to the side of the wall, Zerubbabel sat at a table covered with parchment scrolls. Fragments of old carvings, lilies and pomegranates, were used to hold the scrolls open. On the wall behind Zerubbabel's head were scratched circles and squares, arcs and tangents and all sorts of diagrams.

He looked up from his parchments, a tall grave weary-looking man, his thick beard turning grey. One small lamp burned before him.

"I greet you well, brother," he sad. "I have heard of you. He expects you."

"Who expects me?" asked Blaedud almost in a whisper.

"That Man. Come, I will take you to him."

Bird Caged

On that same evening, Elen after a long and comfortless journey came to a tall stone-built tower. She had been carried behind one of Brogar's horsemen while he himself rode ahead. They were a party of about a score. All day, a cloudy discouraging October day, they had ridden with only short pauses for rest through bare cold country. Brogar had not even let Elen remain behind for Hudibras's funeral but had hurried her to horseback and away from Trinovant, leaving his men behind to take over the fort and the kingdom. Far behind her the sound of the lament for Hudibras died away. And now, in the evening, they came to Brogar's tower.

It was round, massive and flat topped, built of unshaped stones laid one upon another and held together with lime, so that from a distance it glimmered white. A lintelled doorway led to the interior which was like a hollow barrel with a roof above. Torches fixed to the curving wall gave light and by this she could see that a narrow stairway, protected only by posts and rails, led circling up inside the wall to a doorway above.

"Up this way, my lady," said Brogar without ceremony as they lifted her down from the horse.

"Up there? I can't. I should fall over."

"That's easily remedied," he said, and without a word more lashed her wrists to the back of the belt of the man who had carried her. The man walked up the narrow stairway and Brogar came close behind. She could not help but go up the stairs. She submitted in angry scornful silence though her legs, stiff from the long ride, trembled under her. Once she looked down and giddiness overcame her and she fell on the steps. Brogar and the serving-man jerked her to her feet and propped her up till she reached the doorway above. Inside was a small round room, barely furnished. Brogar loosed her wrists and let her sink down on a wooden bench. There was not much in his manner now of the courteous and attentive knight he had formerly seemed.

The rest of the band remained below, but Brogar stood by her till the serving-man had gone out of another door to a chamber further up and returned with the little Lir.

He came running into Elen's arms. He was pale, dirty, unkempt and red-eyed.

"Oh, mother!" he cried. "Have you come to take me away? Oh, do take me away. I don't like it here. It's cold and dark and—I haven't had much to eat." His voice shook and then broke into sobs. She gathered him into her arms.

"Why, yes, my darling, I'll take you away. Indeed I will, as soon as this—this nobleman lets me."

Lir turned his head and looked at Brogar.

"This nobleman? But this is Uncle Brogar, isn't it? But he's different, he's changed. I don't like him . . . Mother, what does he want?"

"Ask him," she said, tight-lipped.

"What do you want—sir?"

"My boy," said Brogar, putting on his wolfish smile, "I want this lady, your mother, to marry me."

"Oh, but no!" exclaimed Lir. "She can't do that. Mother, you can't do that. You're married to my father, who is Prince Blaedud. He'll come back, I know he will. Oh, you couldn't, you couldn't? Tell me you couldn't?"

"No, my darling, be assured," she said, holding him tightly to her. "I can't and I won't. It may cost us dear, but I won't."

"Then *that's* all right," said the boy. "My grandfather the King won't let it happen. He'll come after us with his army as soon as he knows."

"My boy," said Brogar, "your grandfather the King is dead. And your father Prince Blaedud may be dead also for all we know. So now you are the King of the Trinovantes. I wish to be your guardian till you come of age, and protector of your lady mother."

The boy turned to Elen again, pressing close to her and looking up in her face.

"Mother, is this true?"

"It's true, my son, that King Hudibras is dead. It's true that your father has not yet returned. Your father is King now and I am sure he is not dead. But this man wants to make himself king. He would seize me and make himself king according to the old law—and what would become of you, my little son, the Gods only know."

"But my father will come back, won't he?"

"Indeed and indeed he will. And if he did not I would not submit to this man or let him lay a finger on you."

Brogar stood by smiling.

"Is that your answer then, Lady Elen?"

"That is my answer."

"You don't trust me. That is very foolish of you. But I think you may change your mind. Good night to you," and he turned and went out of the door. The serving-man followed him, setting down a rushlight on the table and a small bag of provisions. Then he too went out and bolted the door behind him. They heard the grate of the iron as the bolts went home, receding footsteps, and then silence.

Pythagoras At Last

Zerubbabel led Blaedud along the dark echoing corridors of the unfinished Temple. The moonlight darted eerily in through high windows and distant clerestories, making the dark shadows below darker. Cloths covered the newly painted capitals and swayed in the night breeze. All was quiet in the great hall itself, where the richly contrasted mosaic pavement was already laid, but somewhere far off the thud and chink of hammers still went on. There were chambers opening out of the great hall and chambers above, with stairs going up, and chambers below, with stairs going down. Blaedud looked about him in wonder.

"This is our great work," said Zerubbabel. "We were warned that you might not know. Seventy years back my people were overswept and carried away captive by the King of Babylon and dwelt in exile and great sorrow. Now the King of Persia, Cyrus (may he be blessed), has allowed us to return and rebuild our City and the Temple of our God."

"And what is the name of your God?"

Zerubbabel stopped and turned, half in and half out of a shaft of moonlight, and laid his finger on his lip.

"Our God has no name. He is—The Lord. What name can one give to That-Which-Is?"

Blaedud pondered this, standing still in the quietness, while the echo of the hammers came faintly and from far below.

"Yet your God must have *some* name—some word by which the priests invoke him?"

"True. There are Names. But those Names are very secret and very powerful, and known only to those—to whom they are known. It is said that there is an Ultimate Name"—and he lowered his voice—"which if spoken would shake the heavens and crack the earth and raise the dead to life."

He walked on again descending the great steps outside the Temple into the many courtyards, where the full moonlight and the soft sounds of the city met them.

"But who," said Blaedud, "*is* this God of yours?"

"He is The One. You should know."

"Yes, I know," said Blaedud, and was silent.

Zerubbabel, after thinking for a few moments, went on.

"But whether He, The One, is the same as the One, the beginning of Numbers, that is worshipped everywhere under many names, or whether He is the Great King above Gods, supreme and obeyed by all the others, or whether He is the Only One and all the rest are but inventions and fables, I do not know. Our priests say He is the Only One and the rest are lies and abominations. I am not so sure. And the man we are going to see—well, what he tells us is not the same as the priests' opinion. So we must say no word. He meets us in secret. He knows the secrets of the builders, without which we could not build the Temple. But he knows other secrets besides."

While they spoke, Zerubbabel had led him a tortuous course through small deserted streets. Now they seemed to be turning back and went down steps into a dark tunnel. Zerubbabel carried a small lantern, which had hardly been apparent while they were in the moonlight, but now it shed a little light before them. They seemed to thread a labyrinth, but Blaedud's sense of direction told him they might have gone back under their former tracks and now be underneath the Temple again.

The Holy City is honeycombed with tunnels and passages and stairways below. Zerubbabel said, "It is old, so old, and men have built and pulled down and built again, and have sunk shafts for water and for defence in war—and for secrets."

They reached a door and Zerubbabel knocked in a peculiar way. The knock was answered from within and the door was opened. There was a small cell, with one lamp burning there, and seated in its light was Pythagoras.

No one could have mistaken him. Not only his great height, his white hair and beard, the transparency of his skin, his piercing blue eyes, but a kind of white radiance that seemed to shine from him, making his long loose white robes seem even whiter and his eyes supernaturally luminous. His long shapely hands were outstretched in welcome —they reached out like pale trees but the fingers' ends were spatulate and strong. His body seemed to shine through his garments as if it were a body of gold. His voice when he spoke was the most beautiful that Blaedud had ever heard.

"Welcome, Aether-Treader," he said. "I have watched you. I know you well."

And Blaedud, looking into that face, somehow felt that he too knew this man well. He fell on one knee and lifted a corner of the white robe to his lips. Pythagoras clasped his hand and raised him to his feet, and the touch went through him like fire.

"There is little need to tell me," Pythagoras said. "You seek wisdom. You know much, and would know more. You are a man after my own heart, and I will teach you."

Captivity

For the first three days food and water were brought to Elen and Lir in their prison, although in diminishing quanties each day, and a grim-faced old slave, who appeared to be deaf and dumb, lighted a small fire for them in a brazier.

The worst was the boredom, the tedium, the ennui of having nothing to do. They sang songs and told stories at first. Elen told long stories and for a while kept Lir happy, but then both her memory and her imagination began to tire and he, an energetic nine-year-old boy, grew restive. He stamped round and round the room, banged with anything he could find to bang, shouted tunelessly, teased and tormented Elen. She bore it, realising how hard it was for him, but her head ached and she longed to sleep and could not. Every day Brogar visited her and asked the same question and got the same reply.

On the fourth day the man did not come to light the fire. They thought he had forgotten and Elen spoke of it to the other surly fellow who brought the food. He gave no answer. When Brogar came, she complained to him. He smiled, said he was sorry and repeated his demand. That was all.

It was very cold, for October was advancing.

The next day there was no food, only water.

"Are you trying to starve us into submission, my lord Brogar?" she asked.

"Oh, my lady, you are being very foolish. Why are you still so obstinate?"

The next day there was no water.

The Brothers

Dardan and Rud came running up the shoulder of the downs together, into the sight of the sea. It lay blue and smiling, for it was one of those calm sunny days of October, just before Samhuinn, when the clouds and cold winds call a truce and the yellow grass and red leaves make a little summer.

"Do you know where we are?" cried Dardan.

"Of course I do," answered Rud, almost shouting. "It's Foam Island, our dear old Foam Island. So *that's* where he has put us! Well, it's a prison right enough, but at least we know our way about it."

Brogar's men had fallen upon them as they were on their way southward to answer that deceptive emergency call, five days before King Hudibras died. (But they did not yet know of his death.) Before the men had blindfolded them, they had caught a glimpse of the foxes' tails they wore pinned in their caps, a badge by which Brogar's men were known. Their captors had hurried them away, on horseback, close hooded, and presently they had felt themselves carried into a boat, ferried over water, carried ashore again. They had been fed, still bound and blindfold, and there was something in the ale they were given to drink which made them sleep. When they woke, without the blindfolds, they were in a small rough hovel with two guards. The others had gone.

"Lord Brogar's orders," they were told. "We're here to look after you. We've got stores here to feed us all until the boat comes back."

"How long will that be then?"

"Oh, maybe days—moons. But you won't get away from here. All right—no good killing us. You'll never get away—this is an island and there's no boat. So you can walk all over the island, run if you want to—you'll have to come back here for your food anyway. But you won't get off this island, not unless you can fly like birds."

So they had explored and found it as the guard had said.

" 'Unless you can fly like birds,' he said," Dardan said. "Rud, do you remember what we used to do here?"

"Do I not? Come on, let's see . . ." and they raced away from their very displeased guard. There was a deep dip in the ground and a cleft where the chalk had split, perhaps three feet across, but with the ease of long practice they leapt it. The other side was a small promontory, a peninsula, not more than a mile each way. They knew it well of old. The guard also knew that the chalk cliffs were sheer all the way round. They could not escape, unless they could fly like birds. The guard grunted and sat down to wait for them.

Looking back, above the head of the guard, Dardan and Rud could see a cluster of stones on the summit, the long-deserted College of Princes, where Ceredig and Syweddyd had taught them and Blaedud.

"Blaedud. I wish we knew where he was."

"Flying, I shouldn't wonder," Dardan chuckled.

"He ought to be back before the Old Man dies."

"Yes, that he ought. It's only too plain, I think, Rud, why that man Brogar's done this to us. The Lady Elen."

"Damn the man, yes. And we not there to prevent it. Too easy. Dardan, we must get back, and quickly."

"Oh yes, but—'Unless you can fly like birds'—Rud, do you think it's still there?"

"Come on, let's see."

The down was thickly dotted with gorse bushes, now dry and brown and full of crackling pods but still blooming here and there. Towards the extremity of the little peninsula the bushes thickened into a dense mass, more than head high. Remembering old landmarks, they crashed their way through.

"This was where he made us take the oath of secrecy," Rud remarked.

"Good old Blaedud—well, we've kept it."

They came out into the little dell where the cave was. The cave was still there, its mouth closed with the dead bushes they had piled there. Inside was a mound of silver sand, which they well remembered having heaped there with sacks and spades. Under the sand was a large object wrapped in tarred cloth, and this they dragged out to the light and carefully unwrapped. There it was—the last flying machine they had made before Blaedud was called from Foam Island to his marriage.

"Look, Rud. It's all here. Most of it's still sound. It's not much different, after all, from the later ones we made. The canvas hasn't rotted—we soaked it well with linseed oil. The ropes are still sound too—here, pull this one. The members might be a trifle brittle—we could splint them with reeds if we could get some."

"I've seen a bed of reeds over by the north-west shore. We can tell the guards we want to make fishing rods. They'll laugh."

"Why, I believe it could be done."

In three days it was done. The guards cared very little what their prisoners did, being sure they had no means of getting off the island.

So on a fine morning, for the late fair weather still held, they stood at the edge of the promontory with the contrivance ready.

"One of us must go and the other push him off. We'll cast lots."

"We've no dice," said Dardan. "Tell you what we'll do—each grab a handful of pebbles and count how many. The one that has an odd number of pebbles is the one to go."

So it was done, and Dardan had the odd number.

The promontory faced eastward, and to their north was the British coast, stretching far in both directions. The water here was only a shallow channel and sometimes it was possible to swim it, but only at the right times, otherwise the currents were known to be treacherous, and there were rumours of quicksands. Due north a great estuary opened up and boats could get in and out, and there was a road through the forests to the hinterland. Further east, round the turn of the promontory, was deeper water as the colour of it showed, and south-east and south was the full channel, deep and often stormy, with nothing till one came in sight of the Gaulish coast. But with the wind blowing steady from the south the flying machine might skim safely over to the northward shore, and perhaps even make the estuary.

"We'll pray to the Winds and to the powers of the Air," said Dardan, and so they prayed.

Out of sight the guard, very bored with his task, squatted in the dry grass by the gap.

Rud and Dardan went about their preparations coolly and deliberately.

"I shall go up the river till I meet the high ridgeways," said Dardan. "With luck, the machine might even take me up over the first range of hills. Anyhow I'll try to get to Trinovant and see what's happening. I'll see the Lady Elen safe, and her children. I think Edra will be taking care of the children. And when I can I'll send a boat to get you—I hope they won't avenge my escape on you," he added.

"If they do it can't be helped. We have to think of Elen first. In any case, you'll look after my wife Gwen, and the little ones?"

"Sure I will. Now, no more words. Let's be going."

With a final look to the direction of the wind as it bent grass and bushes, Dardan took his place in the machine— sitting, not hanging by his hands—and Rud launched him off over the edge of the cliff.

The wind took him and lifted him—he was airborne! Up he went and shouted for the joy of his flight. Higher and higher—and then a cloud from the north rapidly mounted the sky, and from it came a violent gust. Rud saw the machine change direction and spin out southwards. It tilted and rocked—it was away out over the full channel now, over the deep water, and the squall rapidly over-shadowing the sky was whipping the waves into grey breakers. The machine seemed to struggle—something was broken—it crumpled in the sky, and fell. It went down, a heap of wreckage, into the heaving waters.

Rud stood watching in horror, and then cried aloud in extremity of grief, a wordless rending cry. Then crouching low to the ground he lamented,

"Oh Dardan, my brother, my brother . . ."

His mind and eyes clouded with grief, he rushed to the side of the cliff and went clambering down it, where no man in his sober senses would dare risk his neck. He threw off his clothes as he went and crashed regardless of pain over the low rocks at the promontory's foot into the sea and, hardly aware if it were suicide, or a hopeless attempt to join his brother, or a wild bid to escape, he struck out across the narrow channel. The guard saw him from the hill above and sent an arrow after him, but he was out of range. He went on, not really knowing what he did, swim-ming towards the British shore and the great river.

Signal and Departure

Blaedud was given a modest and quiet lodging not far from the secret doorway into Pythagoras's grotto. His host, who lived alone with no woman, was one of the Pythagoreans but, being also an Israelite, kept it secret. He knew of the underground way, though he had never been there. Each day a junior disciple came for Blaedud and led him to the grotto. Sometimes Pythagoras was there, sometimes not, sometimes he would come in after Blaedud had arrived—but nobody knew where he went when he was not teaching in the secret place.

The Israelites, Hebrews or Jews, as they were variously called, divided their days into seven, an arrangement Blaedud had not met before. His host told him it was in honour of the seven Planets, which were the dwelling places of the seven great Spirits of God, under whom the world is divided. "But as a Jew," he said, "we must not say that. We are told that it is because The Lord, who is One and Alone, made the world and all in it in six days and rested on the seventh. However it may be, the seventh day—Saturn's—is the day of rest, as Saturn is the planet who is the giver of rest. But I must not say so outside these walls."

So Pythagoras told Blaedud that he would instruct him for six days, and then he must rest on the seventh and think over what he had learnt, and then for six days he should come again for instruction, and it would be seen at the end of that time whether he were ready for the secret that he desired, the secret that would give all men the power of flight.

Blaedud slept in a clean bare little cell. Each night his mind was set at rest by what he had learnt that day from Pythagoras and by the proper spiritual exercises. And for six nights he slept soundly. But on the seventh night his sleep was troubled. He dreamt he was flying—he often dreamt so and enjoyed long dream-flights with the Bird-Woman, though he always knew when it was a dream and not a real journey. But this time Dardan was beside him.

"Why, what are you doing here, you old rascal?" he exclaimed.

"Flying with you, of course—what else?"

"But how did you get here? You never did before."

"Never mind that. But you must get home, Blaedud, you must get home. Elen needs you—you must get home." Dardan placed his hands on Blaedud's shoulders, shaking him and looking into his face with frightening earnestness. Blaedud felt the weight on his chest and awoke gasping and sweating.

It was still dark but he could not sleep again.

This being the first day of the next series of seven, he waited impatiently till the young man came to lead him to the secret grotto.

"You are troubled," Pythagoras said, not a question but a statement. Blaedud hardly needed to tell him but did tell him every detail of his dream as far as he could remember it.

"We will look into a mirror," Pythagoras said, and took from a casket not a mirror but a strange object, a flat disc of black stone, smooth but not bright. It was perfectly circular and set into a silver frame with a handle, like a woman's looking-glass.

"Hold it in your hand," Pythagoras said, "and look steadily."

They were alone in the close little cell far below the Temple—Blaedud seemed to feel the awesome weight of the earth above them. One small lamp flame lit the yellow walls, the rough wooden table with a great parchment unrolled upon it, the white robes and remote unearthly face of Pythagoras. Blaedud's eye strayed towards his teacher's.

"Do not look at me," came the deep soft voice. "Look in the mirror."

And a curtain drew aside within the circle of the black stone and Blaedud saw Elen's face, pale, tear streaked, her yellow hair dishevelled, her lips white. Another face came close to hers—it was young Lir and he was crying. Elen's voice seemed to come from far away. "Help us, Blaedud, help us—it will be too late . . ."

His hand shook, and Pythagoras quickly took the mirror from him or he would have dropped it.

"I must go," Blaedud said. "Oh, but Master—six days more? No, not six days more. Not one day. Not though it were to learn the secret . . . and yet . . . Master?"

Tortured with doubt, he looked into the luminous blue eyes. Pythagoras did not answer.

"Oh, you will surely say—I have heard it said—you will say 'You must give up wife and children for me'—the true initiates have done so—must I? Oh Master, tell me, what must I do?"

"I think you have your answer," said Pythagoras.

"Have I? Oh, but have I?"

"Yes. Think." The blue eyes pierced his. "There have been those to whom The Wisdom was more than love or human feeling or earthly ties. For such as these, it is right that they should cut themselves off from human life. For you, no. You are called to search for knowledge, not for The Wisdom. Knowledge for the attainment of an end, for the benefit it may bring, not only to yourself but to others. And even that is less to you in the end than love. For you, that is the path. The way of love and service. That is the way for you in this life of your many lives. So go home, my son, where you are needed."

Blaedud, the tension relaxed, sank down and sat on the floor at the sage's feet. The Master laid a consoling hand on his head.

"I shall regret you, and miss you, my son. But you must go at once. And how will you go? By the way you came? Treading the Aether?"

Blaedud looked up. "Of course. It's the only way I can go. There isn't a moment to lose. But I can't do it unless She helps me. Do you think She will?"

Pythagoras smiled sadly.

"She may be willing—or not. She is not one of the Great Powers but a spirit of the Kingdom of the Air, having a human heart but not yet a human soul. She is subject to the passions. She is jealous."

"I know, I know—but oh, Master! She *must* help me! What shall I do if she will not?"

"Come," said Pythagoras, "there are means we may use to conjure her. It may be for her good as well as yours. But not in this place."

When the sun was at its height Blaedud met with Pythagoras, as he had appointed him, outside the City on a bare and stony hillside overlooking a sheer precipitous drop. It was a desert spot where no one was likely to disturb them. Blaedud brought with him his kite, trimmed and repaired for a journey, and was clothed ready to go.

"We must work in the Element of Air," Pythagoras said, "and under the rulership of Mercury. So let us begin and make our conjuration."

With the sun beating down upon them and the shrill dry sound of the grasshoppers all about them in the crackling weeds, the philosopher drew the circle with his long staff and traced the figures within it. He began to speak words, soft pattering muttering words. It was as if the silence, the sun, the grasshoppers' sound, stretched like a cord, tighter and tighter. Then he raised his voice and sent one great awesome sound ringing out, breaking the silence, snapping the cord. And after that great syllable he called,

"Thou Spirit of Air, appear before me. I command thee, in that Name which thou knowest, appear before me and obey me. FIAT! FIAT! FIAT!"

She did not come flying, as Blaedud expected, but she glimmered into sight, in the shimmering of the air above the heated ground. Fluttering and quivering in all her feathers, at first transparent, then crystalline, she took shape out of the moving air. She seemed to struggle, as if she came unwillingly.

"I hear and obey, O Master of Spirits," she said. "What do you command me?" Blaedud had never heard her voice so soft and submissive.

Pythagoras, his white robes full of the noonday light, his white hair vibrant, leaned upon his staff and looked at her gently but with power.

"I could commande thee, Spirit of Air, but I will compel thee more powerfully. Do you love this mortal?"

"I do, Master of Spirits."

"Then you will take him and convey him safely over land and sea to his wife and children, and aid him for their safety."

She turned her face aside, jerking her head like a petulant child.

"Must I?" She spoke unwillingly. "Must I take him back to—her?"

"If you love him, yes."

"But I *do* love him!" Never before had Blaedud seen the blackness of her eyes nor how they could spark with anger. "I, I myself—*I* love him and he's mine, not hers. I wanted to give him the secret of flight—here and now, not hundreds of years hence. But she drags him back. She always

128

drags him back. Why must he go back to her now? The secret is within his grasp."

"Spirit of Air, you forget that the secret is in my gift."

"And haven't I prepared him for you, and brought him to you for this very thing? And must he throw it away now?"

"If I do not choose to give it him yet, what is that to thee, Spirit of Air? And if he chooses of his own will to turn back now, for love, cannot you aid him—for love?"

She was silent and her rainbow wings drooped. Presently she said,

"I thought I understood love . . . Perhaps I do not yet."

"Perhaps you begin to. Oh, Spirit of Air, is it possible that the beginnings of a human soul may stir in you?"

A light dawned in her eyes. "A human soul? Master of Spirits, you know my longing—look, there are tears in my eyes. Shall I give up my own dearest desire, to buy—tears?"

"Do so, Spirit—for tears are precious."

"Then I will do it," she said.

Pythagoras stretched out his hand over her.

"May you have peace, Spirit. And because you give him up now, your time shall come to possess him. Go now, in the name of Mighty Hermes, who keeps the paths of the sky. Go, and may the One Above All be above you, and protect you."

Breaking Point

Lir had ceased to be boisterous. He sat against the wall, his head pressed against his upraised knees. Elen, beside him, drew him against her and wrapped her cloak around him, but when he took any notice of her at all it was to shake her off. Their prison was desolately cold.

Then, on the fifth morning, there was a change. Two women entered and put a cup of warmed milk to Elen's lips, and to Lir's. Her first thought was that it was poisoned, but now she did not care. Let her go. Let them both die together and be done with it. So she drank, but it did not seem to be poisoned. It was laced with wine and honey and some strength began to come back to her. She looked around—men had come in and were setting up a bed, a great curtained bedstead with a big soft feather mattress. Others brought a tub and filled it with warm scented water and then retired. The women gently bathed them both and clad them in warm shifts of white wool and laid them side by side in the bed. Bewildered and relaxed, they dropped off to sleep.

When they woke, the women helped them from the bed to a table by the side of a warm brazier, where an appetizing meal was served to them. Elen ate as in a dream, wondering if she were indeed already dead and in heaven. Lir attacked the meal eagerly, but was after all not well enough to eat much. But he sat back in the fur rugs in which they had wrapped him and seemed drowsily content.

And then Brogar came in.

He was smiling, courteous, pleasant.

"You are kind, my lord," said Elen.

"Who would not be, lady? See, I can be as kind as this, and kinder. Will you not yield to me now?"

"No!" she cried, springing from her chair and throwing the furs away from her. "Neither for your cruelty nor for your kindness. No and no and no!"

"Oh, you are a very obstinate lady, and a very foolish one. You don't believe your Blaedud will come and rescue you now? If he's alive, he's away overseas with his winged goddess. He is not true to you, lady."

"And that is a lie," she flung at him. "You and your creature Ragan—lies you have made up between you. Not one word do I believe of anything you tell me. You cannot make me yield that way."

"Then, lady, I am sorry." He turned to the door and made a signal to the men who were waiting outside. They came in and began to carry things out. Brogar took Elen's arm and led her to the other stairway, the one that went upward, one of the men following behind with Lir. "It is regrettable, but this chamber is required for other uses. This is all I can give you now," and he led them out into the keen night air on to the roof of the tower.

A small circular space, bare to the stars, was encircled by a breast-high wall. There was no shelter of any kind. The frost lay heavy on the stones.

"So, lady, I must bid you good night," he said. "Unless you change your mind."

And the door clanged behind him, the bolts ground home, and the steps went away down the winding staircase.

Elen caught Lir to her and shielded him from the cold as best she could. "Oh, my child, my child," she moaned. "How could he? How could he? What is to become of us now? Oh, Blaedud—come to me, come to me, for this is my last need!"

The dark cold hours passed. Lir was in a high fever now, and raved, sometimes imploring his mother to surrender and let them get away and then, in almost the same instant, cursing and defying her and commanding her not to yield.

"Oh Gods, this will be his death," she said. "Oh Blaedud, Blaedud, wherever you are—my own life is nothing. I'd gladly die to keep my faith with you, but I can't let your son die."

She crept to the wall and looked down. Far below she could see a sentinel's fire. She called as loudly as she had the strength.

"Oh, you below there—you below there!"

The man heard her and came nearer, with a torch in his hand.

"You called, lady?"

"I called. Summon the lord Brogar. Tell him I yield."

It seemed a long time but at length she stood again in the turret room, holding Lir in her arms. There was no little weight to him now.

Brogar was sitting very much at his ease by the brazier. He stood up, courteously enough, as the men brought them in.

"My lord, it is enough. I yield. I cannot risk the boy's life."

"Why, that's my girl!" (She winced at the familiarity.) "Now, that's a lady of sense. We'll bring back all the comforts, and tomorrow we'll set off back to Trinovant."

"But I make conditions," she said.

"Oh, how so? What conditions?"

"You will swear to me that the boy shall not be harmed. And you will not lay a finger on me till we are lawfully wedded in the face of all the people. For if these things are not done, I will die. I will find means to kill myself—and, my lord, in such a way as to let my people, and my father's people, know that you have caused my death."

"How would you do that?" he said frowning.

"I am not telling you how, but I will do it. So, swear to me that you will not touch me till we are publicly married—else, you know, you cannot claim the kingdom—and swear that no harm shall come to Lir or to my other children."

"Well, since you will have it so."

"Then I will do as you wish. But let this poor child be seen to, if you have any human compassion in you at all."

The Kingdom of the Air

The start of the flight was pure pleasure. Out over the cliff edge, needing no pushing, the Bird-Woman's great wings behind him, the kite taking the air smoothly, firmly, rising up on the warm current that lifted it like a strong and steady hand. Blaedud had no fear or hesitation. He felt no vertigo as he looked back and saw the white figure and radiant face of Pythagoras. A wave of strength and confidence seemed to come from that face and those upraised hands. The white figure grew smaller and smaller—the wilderness stretched out, mud coloured and wrinkled—the Holy City could be seen far off, like a child's toy—no, smaller—then only as a patch of lighter colour. And the blue layers of air thickened above it.

Blaedud looked up towards the sky and sang as he soared like a skylark.

"Elen, Elen—I'm coming to you, I'm coming, coming, coming—"

"Save your breath," came the Bird-Woman's dry voice over his shoulder. "You'll need it."

Noon had passed and the sun was westering. They turned westward, and then Blaedud gasped and ceased his song abruptly as he saw what was before him.

A solid wall of cloud, slate coloured, shutting out the sun—below it was a clear band of light, yellowish and stormy, crossed with streaks of rain. Above, the upper edge of the slate-coloured pall broke into billowing curves, piling up into the heights, castle above castle of round rolling shapes, with here and there an edge, an outline, of dazzling light where the sun caught it, and across the slate-coloured mass passed, from minute to minute, rapidly moving wisps of white vapour like steam from a cauldron.

"Must we go under that?" Blaedud whispered over his shoulder to the Bird-Woman, his eyes upon the band of lurid yellow light beneath the great cloud.

"Under it? No, no—we must go over it. If we went *under* it, the lightning would mash us into the ground. Go up—go up—higher, higher—"

He pulled the controls that tilted the edge of the kite upward, and the kite soared—away and over—higher than he had ever flown before. His ears sang and popped, and a cruel pressure built up in them till he felt as if his head would burst.

And then they were up and over the cloud castles, and before Blaedud there stretched what looked to him like a long smooth level floor. Piles of white cloud stood in orderly lines, motionless in long symmetrical rows like an army marshalled for hosting. Though it was no solid floor they stood upon, yet they were cut off in a straight line below, as if indeed they stood on a firm surface—blue lanes, bordered by white pillars. He laughed and drove on down the straight blue avenue. And then he was conscious of Dardan flying beside him, just as in his dream.

He saw Dardan's face quite plainly, but all the rest was somehow hidden in mist or vagueness.

"Why, Dardan, you again?" he exclaimed. "What are you doing here?"

"Flying, of course, can't you see?" laughed Dardan, grinning with pure happiness.

"But how did you get here? Have you grown wings, or what?"

"I don't know—don't ask me. But I've come to give you warning. It's Elen. You must go to her at once. She's in danger."

"I know—you came and told me before—but that was a dream, I thought. Isn't this a dream too? No matter—who threatens her?"

"A—a man. I can't think of his name. Funny, I can't remember names now."

"But you remember your name and mine, and Rud's—where's Rud?"

"Ah, poor Rud. No, I don't know. I had to leave him behind."

"Dardan . . ." A suspicion, a fear, came into his mind. "Dardan, are you dead?"

"Am I dead? What is that—dead? I don't understand. I don't know. But I do know you must hurry to Elen."

"I'm coming as quick as I can."

"But not quick enough. Oh, why are you fettered to that silly machine? I've found out a better way. Leave the machine and come with me. It's much quicker and easier. Come!"

Blaedud's hands were on the straps that bound him in his swing chair. But the Bird-Woman's hands, hard as talons, clutched his shoulders.

"No," she said. "No, you don't. Not yet. This isn't the time. Sit still, and mind the machine. We must go higher yet."

They soared, and somehow Dardan dropped away behind them.

Out of the blue transparency below them, among the white masses of cloud, were suddenly white and brown pylons of rock and ice. The kite was racing towards them, or the peaks were racing towards the kite. Blaedud could feel the crash coming . . .

"Up and over," said the Bird-Woman. "Dodge them if you can't overpass them. So—so—now up—up—"

Once again they were going towards the underside of massive cloud towers. The sinking sun lit the undersurfaces with red but above was vast darkness. Suddenly they were into the darkness and a white hissing river of lightning split the cloud before them. At the same time a wind seized the kite and spun it vertiginously round, out of all control. Through the turbulence he still heard the Bird-Woman's voice.

"Hold on. Hold hard. I'm with you. Let it take you, you won't fall. Only hold on."

He held on, battered, deafened, spun about, shaken beyond consciousness. The lightning hissed and darted all round him and the thunder bellowed till his benumbed ears could only feel it rather than hear it. Every hair on his head and body stood upright with the electrical force pouring out of it. And now a kind of madness that was beyond fear possessed him. Out of the clouds, momentarily lit by the lightning, came horrible shapes, bearing down on him—coiling beasts, with long necks and batlike wings, great eyes and terrible faces—shapes that had no faces, only clusters of writhing legs—long undulating worm shapes—thin bony rattling things—all these, crushed together, crowded together, writhing together, all carried on the tide of the noise, the intolerable noise of the thunder . . .

And then, overshadowing, overbearing, overcoming all of them, one vast dark presence—a shape too big, too big to be tolerated, too vast for human endurance, something of a human face, but hideous—it seemed as if the blue-black of the night sky were shaped into a devouring mouth that opened for him . . .

"Go-on," he heard the Bird-Woman say "Right in. Yes, into the mouth of That One."

And with his last ounce of resolution and strength, Blaedud steered his craft into the mouth of Old Night, past the devouring teeth, into the throat that was darkness of darkness . . .

And was suddenly out into a clear blackness full of stars. Full of huge stars, but otherwise—nothing. Nothing. Silence, and the utter nakedness between the worlds. Under the eyes of the stars and the silence, there he was.

Nothing that he had been through terrified him more than that.

Extremity

Brogar's castle stood on one of the ridges of high ground between the valley of the Tamis and the southern sea. He had taken Elen there, by hard riding, in less than a night and a day, but coming back the progress had to be slower. There had to be a hand litter for Lir, who was recovering but still too weak to leave his bed. And Elen could not ride very vigorously. So the calvacade proceeded at a slow pace and broke the journey at one of Brogar's villages on the high downs. Quarters were found for Elen and Lir in a sufficiently comfortable hut belonging to the chief of the village, and the chief's wife and daughters waited on them assiduously. Brogar was courtesy and consideration itself, but Elen kept him at arm's length and would not let him set foot inside the hut. The village chief's wife, a stout and formidable woman, mounted guard inside the door of the hut and there was no getting past her without violence that would have outraged the village.

In the morning, a grey chilly morning now nearing November, close on the dread day of Samhuinn, when the dead mingle with the living, when the beasts are killed for the winter and a shudder comes over men at the knowledge of the grim days that lie ahead—in this grey morning the calvacade assembled to resume their march. There was Brogar at the head and beside him, on a low pony, was Elen, wrapped in a long cloak. She would not have been easy to recognise—her once smooth yellow hair, before she drew the hood over it, was rough, dull and lack-lustre. Her beautiful face was grey and pinched and she sat drooping and round-shouldered, without life or lightness. Behind her came Brogar's two women-servants on their ponies and then Lir in his litter, carried by four strong serfs, and then the rest of Brogar's bodyguard. The curtains of the litter were closed but, before mounting, Elen had anxiously looked inside to see if Lir was there, for she still feared treachery. He looked up at her sleepily and gave her a reassuring smile. His fever had gone and if it did not return he would be well.

"I was good and ate my frumenty," he told her. "We're going home, aren't we?"

"Oh yes, my darling, we're going home." She closed the curtains and went back to her horse, but with her heart reproaching her. The boy did not know yet that she had consented to marry Brogar. How would he take it? Would the shock make him ill again, perhaps drive him out of his mind? His hold on life was still so frail . . .

The villagers had turned out to see the visitors depart. Among them was a group of beggars, clamorous and unsightly.

"Why do you have so many beggars?" she asked Brogar. "In Hudibras's kingdom we did not have any, nor in my father's."

"Oh," he said, sweeping his whip at them, "they're all fools and rogues. Fools who wouldn't pay my taxes, so what could I do but take their houses and cattle. And bad men, criminals. They had to be punished." And with horror she saw that some of them were minus hands or eyes.

"Oh, give them the broken meats that we left," said Brogar to his attendants. "And then whip them off. Come, lady, are you ready?"

And then a man ran forward out of the crowd of beggars. He was naked but for a tatter of dirty rags. His tow-coloured hair and beard were streaked and matted, his back and breast and arms were all scarred and scratched—but she recognised his face. It was Rud.

"Lady—" he began, but she put her finger to her lips. A kind of instinctive impulse such as comes to an animal in danger prompted her. On a bench by the door of the hut where they had lodged, someone had left a knife. With her eyes and a hardly perceptible movement of her fingers, she directed his eyes to it. Quickly he snatched it up and hid it in his rags.

"What's this?" said Brogar, turning suddenly. "You filthy rogue, what are you doing here? You're molesting the lady. Guards, take this fellow to the back and hang him."

"No, no!" Elen shrieked. "Not that, not that! Lord Brogar, no! He's no rascal. Brogar, don't you recognise him? This is Rud, King Hudibras's son, my lord's brother—"

"Is he so?" said Brogar, with an evil smile. "Why, lady, that's a very good reason I should keep him in safety. Take care of him, then," he commanded the guards, "and don't hurt him, but bind his feet and bring him along. I'll—give you further instructions about him later. Now, Lady Elen, before we go, I have a pleasant surprise for you."

"A pleasant surprise?" she asked bleakly.

"Yes. I have secured a splendid nurse for our little Lir. The very best—here she is," and from the crowd stepped out Ragan.

"Oh, not her, not her!" The thought went through Elen's mind—this is Lir's death warrant.

"Why, but lady—why are you so foolish? You know her—she nursed the King and eased his pain, you trusted her—" (Yes, to my sorrow, thought Elen.) "Then let's have no more words."

"I won't let her touch him." Leaving the side of her horse, Elen ran back to the litter and stood between Ragan and the curtains. Ragan, reaching past her, snatched the curtains back and looked in. The boy gave a shriek.

"That woman! Mother, mother, don't let her come near me! She's a witch—"

Brogar, with a snarl of impatience, sprang from his horse and laid a rough hand on Elen's shoulder.

But at that moment a shout arose,

"Look in the sky! Look in the sky! The gods, the gods! A bird, a man, a spirit, a fiend—*look in the sky!*"

And through the rent clouds a kite-shaped black form, wide winged, menacing, without sound like a ghost, swept down upon them. Villagers, men-at-arms, all of them, ran here and there or cowered upon the ground. And Elen watched in amazement as Blaedud, swooping in magnificent motion, descended.

One man did not cower. Brogar snatched a bow from one of his terrified followers, fitted an arrow to it and aimed, as the great undefended form of the Bird-Man came nearer. It was a perfect target—an easy shot—he couldn't miss—

Then a quick movement from behind. Elen, in fascinated horror, saw the tow-headed beggarman break from his guards and, before the arrow could be loosed, plunge that knife deep into Brogar's back. Brogar fell and in the same instant Blaedud's flying feet touched the ground, he cast himself off quickly from the machine, and ran.

As the astonished men-at-arms hurried to the side of their chief, Blaedud clasped Elen to him, and sent his voice ringing.

"I am come, I am come—Elen, my love, I Blaedud, am come flying, out of the realms of the air! I, Blaedud the King, am come flying and let no man oppose me now, for this is my hour! Oh Elen, my love, my love!"

LAST FLIGHT OF ALL

Happy Home

". . . So now you know," Blaedud said to Elen, "how it was between me and the Bird-Woman—all of it, my dear." She nestled close to him. They were sitting comfortably in their own great hut, in a nest of rugs, furs, sheepskins and cushions, with a glowing brazier in front of them. The other side of the brazier the three children huddled together in another nest and played knucklebones. Outside the bitter rain of winter lashed down, but here they were warm and happy.

"It was that woman Ragan," she went on. "I should not have trusted her. From the moment I saw her exchange looks with Brogar, I knew how it was. And now I know how she betrayed you at the first . . . What has become of her? Did they kill her?"

"No, no, my love. I am unwilling to do such a thing. My reign is to be a reign of mercy, as far as in me lies. I have banished her and she is far enough away by now. I think the powers to whom she has given herself will deal with her in due time. But can you indeed bring yourself to understand about the Bird-Woman? Bless you, dear heart."

"I owe your life to her," she said. "Mine too, for I would not have lived . . . Blaedud, how did you part from her?"

"Well, now," he said, looking ashamed, "I'm sorry to say I never said good-bye to her at all. It was all so strange and dreamlike—when I came through the clouds and saw you, there was no time—and after that, she was gone. It was ungrateful of me, but she didn't wait to be thanked.

When the rain has gone and the weather is better, I'll make a shrine to her on top of this hill, the Hill of Troy-Town, and offer sacrifices."

"Oh yes—what shall we offer? What would she like, do you think? A lovely white lamb, as soon as the lambs are born, or a pair of white doves—"

"No, we won't offer anything like that. I know she wouldn't want a blood sacrifice. The followers of Pythagoras never made blood sacrifices, though the Israelites in their great Temple were never done with pouring out the blood of bulls and goats. The whole place stank of blood." He shuddered. "Yet it was very holy . . . The Greeks made blood sacrifices too, to their Gods and Goddesses, but not the Pythagoreans. They offered flowers, and honey, and milk, and fruit. And that is what we will offer to the Bird-Woman."

He was silent in thought for a while and then went on as if it were thinking aloud.

"There are many changes I must make. Things I have learnt that I must use here. They—the philosophers—they worship the God of Light—we can call Him the Sun, for it is the same Bright One that the Druids teach our people to worship, though the Greeks give Him the name of Phoebus Apollo. He is light and music and healing and all goodness. We will build him a temple down by the river, where the town is beginning to grow. It shall be a temple of stone, with pillars and porticoes like those in Greece." He looked round him. "I'd like different houses, too. Out there they had stone houses, with stone floors— even those who were not very rich had them. White and clean and full of light."

She lifted her head from the rugs where they sheltered her from the draughts that poured through the hut.

"All very well, dear, out there in Greece, but think how cold they'd be here!"

"Not so cold," he said. "They keep the wind out better. Means could be found to make them warm. And in the summer they wouldn't get close and stinking and full of creatures."

She laughed gently. "You've certainly got some new

ideas. But don't start making changes too quickly. Not just yet."

"Oh no, my dear, I won't. First of all I want to set up my College."

"Your College? What's that?"

"Why, a school for philosophers. The young Druids, as they grow up. Dear old Ceredig, you tell me, sleeps with his fathers under the mound and poor Syweddyd can't be long in following. But both have sons, there are other young Druids. I should like them to learn the things I learnt overseas. And not only the Druids' sons and the princes. Everybody, everybody who wishes to learn, high and low, rich and poor. Let them all come to my College."

"What, women too?" she asked, smiling.

"Of course—why not, if there are any that want to learn? Yourself, my love, if you wish it."

"Oh, I'm too busy with the children!" she laughed. "Not to mention looking after you. But where will you have this College of yours? Here in Trinovant?"

"No, I think not here. There's a place near my hot springs—you remember? A place that I felt was blessed. Across a ford with stepping-stones there's a green meadow, high and dry. The people call it the Ford of the Stones. That's where my College will be. And I'll send for teachers from overseas and they shall teach my people every kind of learning."

"But—not how to fly?"

"No, I don't think I shall ever fly again."

Fruit of the Years

And so the years passed, winter into summer, Beltane to Lunasagh, to Samhuinn, to Yule, to Imbolc and round to Beltane once more, and on again through many years.

Blaedud carried out at least some of his plans and did

some of the things he meant to do. Remembering how it was among the Pythagoreans in their daily life, he tried to teach his people to be a little more cleanly in their homes, to bury rubbish and ordure, and to keep from polluting the water supplies. He had a stone house built, but with baked tiles on the floor instead of stone flags or trampled earth. In the summer he used linen sheets on the bed and waged war on flies and fleas. People thought him crazy, of course.

But his great College at the Ford of the Stones (later ages, in a very different tongue, called it "Stan-Ford") grew and prospered. Learned men came from Greece and conferred with the new generation of Druids. Blaedud put Rud in charge of the growing town of Troynovant, or Trinovant, while he himself spent much time at the College, learning and disputing with the wise men. In particular he was working out a code of laws. No longer was the kingdom to be governed by the will and pleasure of its ruler, but by laws that were above all rulers. The Israelites had such a law that was above kings. The Athenians had such a law and they appointed a Goddess to defend it— Themis, the Goddess of Law and Right, who was an aspect of the Great Lady. So the sons of Brutus should henceforth have their law, and it should be formulated with the greatest of care under the guidance of the wisest men that could be found. Many came to Britain, only not Pythagoras himself. That would have been too much to expect—and even that "golden Man" must in time grow old. And Blaedud himself and his Elen looked at each other from time to time and counted the grey hairs. Twenty years since he had come flying to claim his kingdom . . . The children grew up, Lir and Bran and Cordeil, handsome youngsters. And in Trinovant the Temple of the Sun stood with its white pillars and bloodless sacrifices were made there daily, while away on the topmost hill above the new town there was a stone laid upon two stones, and there Blaedud would take a garland of clover flowers and poppies, or primroses, or meadowsweet, and a libation of wine, to the Bird-Woman and to the soul of Dardan, who had no known grave.

"Your King Blaedud is growing old," said the strange woman with the brown face and the silver necklaces, who sat under a porch in the market place of Trinovant, near the ale booths. There were many strangers in Trinovant now, for it could call itself a town and a port, and, with all that came and went, no one recognized Ragan. She had never had many friends before her banishment who would remember her now, but she cultivated many new acquaintances. She went from group to group stirring up gossip, stirring up rumours.

"He's not so old," said a woman at her side. "What is he—fifty? Old Hudibras lived to be ninety."

"Ah, yes, but old Hudibras, the Gods be good to him, was twice as vigorous, ten times as vigorous. This man now, he's a weakling."

"Is he indeed?" another woman joined in. "I've not seen it."

"Yes, but how long since you've seen him at all? *I've* seen him, I tell you, and he's growing old, he's weakening. And that isn't good for the kingdom—you know that. The king is the life of the kingdom, and when the king weakens so does the kingdom. Why, haven't you noticed how the seasons aren't as they should be? Call this a summer! Not enough sun to get the hay in and then storms when you should be getting the barley and the wheat in, no matter for all the prayers in the Temple of the Sun."

"Prayers in the Temple of the Sun!" a man broke in. "What's the good of all those prayers without any sacrifice? Not a bullock, not a sheep offered there or anywhere else since this man became king. How can you keep your God happy without blood? No wonder the crops are failing."

"And you never see him," Ragan pursued the subject, "because he's always away at that College of his, over by the Hot Baths. College! Does anybody know what they learn at that College of his? Black sorcery, I shouldn't wonder."

The hearers shuddered. The crowd was large now—all the idlers from the ale booths had joined in.

"And to keep his College going, and his bloodless Temple, you have to pay tribute to him—"

"Oh, it's not as much as in old Hudibras's time," said another woman. "Be fair to him. It's not as much by a long way. And he doesn't spend it all on himself eating and drinking."

"No, he's not man enough to do that," guffawed a big burly smith from the back of the crowd, his stature and voice overtopping the rest. "What's he got—three children? Old Hudibras had forty-five when he died. Six wives he had too, and others as well. That was a man!"

"Not so much of that neither," objected the woman who had spoken in Blaedud's favour. "You all know how much he gives away in the bad winters, and he lets some people off their tax altogether—"

"He never let me off," said the smith, "though trade's cruel bad. Went to him on my bended knees, I did, and all he said was 'You're no object of pity—pay up and look pleasant!' Bah!" He spat.

"And why did you all accept him as your king?" said Ragan, and their eyes were all fastened on her. "Why, because some people told you they'd seen him come flying, out of the clouds like a bird. More than mortal man, they said, flying like a god. Well, has anybody here seen him fly?"

No reply came.

"There, you see. You just believe what people tell you. Flying indeed! Do you believe it?"

"I don't, for one," said the smith.

"Nor I." "Nor I."

"Same as that story about the pigs. Why, do you realize —if that tale were true, he was a leper once. He might be so still for all you know."

"A leper can't be king," said a man who had not spoken before.

"Him and his pigs!" cried another.

"Perhaps his pigs flew," laughed the smith.

"Ho, ho, ho . . ."

A young fellow with a stringed instrument, on the edge of the crowd, struck up a tune and sang,

> "Pigs might fly,
> "and so might I,
> "But I'm a very unlikely bird!"

The crowd took up the lampoon and sang it with delight.

"Tell you what," said the smith, when he could make himself heard, "if he wants us to obey him—pay for his college, follow all his silly notions about cleaning the streets and burying the muck and all that, and his laws too—well, if he wants us to obey him and his laws, let him show us that he really can fly. Let him fly, so that we can see him, all of us, and we'll do what he wants."

A loud clamour of applause showed that the people in the market place agreed. Ragan went on to seek another crowd elsewhere.

And soon the rumor ran up and down the whole kingdom.

"Blaedud! Who's Blaedud?"

"Who's he to tell us what to do?"

"Who's he to ask for taxes?"

"What does he do with them, anyway?"

"Spends them on his College—a lot of foreign priests! What goes on there, we'd like to know!"

"Him and his laws—why, a man can't beat his own wife, let alone kill his own serf—"

"And all that about cleaning the streets and burying the muck—as if it mattered!"

"And never a decent war—"

"They say he came flying like a bird—"

"Flying like a bird! Let us see him fly, then!"

" 'Pigs might fly, and so might I—' "

"Fly, Bird-Man, fly! Let us all see you fly and we'll believe you!"

The rumor grew and surged around the King's great stone house, round the Temple of the Sun God by the river, all down the long road that led to the Baths of Sul and across the stepping-stones to the College.

When Blaedud went out along the road, or into the woods hunting, or over the Hill of Troy-Town and down into the town of Trinovant by the river, there were still cheerful shouting crowds of his people to greet him, but here and there were knots and clumps of men at corners, who raised the cry as he went by,

"Fly, Blaedud, fly!"

At first he shook off the annoyance, but soon it became more than he could shake off. Even Elen could hear them saying,

"Lady, tell him to fly and we'll believe him!"

"These are just a few malcontents here and there," she told Blaedud. "Not very many—you can see them always standing behind the others and whispering. Why don't you tell the guards to seize them and hang them?"

"I would, at the snap of a finger," said Lir, who was now a tall young man, taller than his father but thinner, and with his mother's lint-white hair. "I'd cut off a few heads and that would silence the rest."

"No," said Blaedud, "we don't rule that way. Gently and with mercy."

"I begin to think you are too merciful," said Elen.

Everywhere the cry grew,

"Fly, Blaedud, fly!"

Even those who defended and upheld him would say,

"Of course he can fly. Some day he'll show you all. But it's a long time to wait."

She Never Fails

On the hilltop, above the King's stone house, in a lonely spot was the shrine Blaedud had made for the Bird-Woman. He had not seen her for years, not even in dreams—in fact, not since his great return. Yet he often went up to that high place and paid honour to her.

It was a few days before Midsummer and the sky was cloudless. Noontide had always been the best time to meet the Bird-Woman. It was hot shimmering noon now, the top of the hill blazing with gorse blooms and cracking in the heat. Further down the hill the oak trees were heavy in leaf, but the summit was bare to the skies. Further off was the place where on Midsummer Day the Druids and all the people would greet the sunrise.

He hardly expected she would come to him, but his heart was heavy and his need great. He made the figures and signs as Pythagoras had taught him, lit the small fire and offered flowers and sweet gums and wine, and prayed with all his heart to the One under whom all exists and to Phoebus who manifests the Light on earth and to the ruler of Air in the East—and then he called on her, his Bird-Woman, his mysterious mother.

And, to his surprise, she was there. Just as when Pythagoras had conjured her, she did not come flying but glimmered up into shape out of air. In her spread of rainbow wings, she sat upon the capstone of the trilithon and bent down to him. She was the same as ever, and yet changed—softer, less fierce, and her jet-black hair was touched with silver where the light caught the ripples, like the moonlight on the water.

"Yes," she said, reading his thoughts, "I wear them like a jewel—the grey hairs. For they mean that I am becoming more like humanity. They mean that my soul is growing."

His eyes filled with tears and he could find no words.

She teased him gently.

"You're not so young yourself, come to that. Red-headed as ever, but thicker—for shame, you'll soon have a paunch! Heavier, I'll swear, not the slim little boy I used to carry!"

"Yet you could carry me?" he asked anxiously.

"I can, and I will. I know your need. These people, they will always tempt their Gods. Well, let it be Midsummer Day, at high noon."

The great wings flickered and dissolved away into the shaking air.

Midsummer Eve

The worst was the crash of having nothing to do. They sang songs and told stories at

Great preparations were always made for the day of Midsummer. For this was the day when the Sun, having reached his highest point in the heavens, could go no higher and must start to go down. The sunrise was a solemn moment, greeted by all the tribe on the summit of the hill. Then at noon was the sacrifice and the feast. Although it was known that Blaedud had no love for blood sacrifices, yet he permitted this one, for it was a festival of the people—the oxen whose blood was poured out for the Sun were roasted over great fires and all the people feasted and were merry. In the evening the fires would be built high and young and old would dance round them, and the boys and girls would take hands and leap across them for a pledge of love. And great blazing barrels of tar and pitch would be rolled down the hill, to show the Sun beginning his descent. Many years past, so the story went, a chosen young man used to be placed in the blazing barrel and rolled down the hill to his death, as an offering to the Sun, but not now. No death or terror now, but only joy in the face of the Sun and the love of the Gods.

A great deal to do—bread and ale for the feasters, clean robes and garlands—Elen and her maids had their hands full. In the bustle of the evening before the festival, young Lir was suddenly at his mother's side, pale and breathless.

"Mother—there's something that frightens me. Where is Father?"

Her heart missed a beat but she answered coolly enough, looking up from her breadmaking.

"I don't know, I'm sure—where should he be?"

"It's—the flying-machine, Mother. It's gone from the place where he keeps it locked up. The doors are open and it's gone. No, it's not been broken into—everything is in good order and there're wood chips and scraps of cord on the ground as if—as if he'd been working on it."

She left the baking bench. "Oh, Lir—you don't think he's going to try to fly again? Because of the people urging him? Oh, Lir, no!"

"Mother, I'm afraid it's so. It looks like it. We don't know where he's gone or where he's taken the kite. But we'll have to find him and stop him. He mustn't do it."

"Oh no, he mustn't do it! The people plague him and torment him and threaten him—but he mustn't be allowed to. Where is Rud? He might know where he is."

But Rud had no knowledge of where he had gone, only he was confident no harm would come.

"He'll be back, dear Lady Elen—why, he always comes back. And if he does try to fly once more, I'm sure he'll come to no harm. His Goddess will protect him. Have faith."

"You've more faith than I have, dear Rud," she smiled at him. But though he spoke confidently, he thought of Dardan.

But Blaedud returned late that night and slipped quietly into bed, taking Elen in his arms. She cried herself to sleep against his shoulder, though indeed she did not know why.

Zenith

Midsummer morning. The clear blue sky with the light gradually growing, the full moon high in the west, a pale disc on the blue. Long streaks of mist over the eastern point and a red light growing behind them. All over the hill the people were quietly assembling. The procession of the Druids came slowly up, their white robes spectral in the dimness. They went through the solemn movements of their rite. Then, as the sun's disc showed itself, the bronze trumpets rang out and all the people hailed the Sun.

There was a pause after the shout had died away and from out of the middle of the crowd, where he had been standing unnoticed, Blaedud stepped forth and stood on the summit of the hill. His red hair, in which the early sunlight found out the gold and not the grey, was circled with his royal coronet. His long dark robe fell to his feet, a solemn shape. Over the heads of the crowd his voice rang out.

"People of the Trinovantes, hear me, your King. Some of you say I am no longer fit to rule. Some of you do not believe that I came among you flying, or that I could fly again."

A murmur arose as of conflicting voices.

"Then behold me. Have it as you wish. Today I will fly, for all of you to see. Today at the time of the noonday sacrifice. That is my word."

He wrapped his cloak around him and turned away, striding back to his own house.

High noon had come. The sun blazed down upon the heath and gorse of the high place and dried the yellow grass. All the tribe were there, and strangers from other tribes and from far away, to see the marvel. This was always a day for every man, woman and child to be present, for it was a great and happy feast, but this time a wonder was to be seen.

Over all the great slope of the hill the people were spread and there were trestle tables where bread and ale would be set out, and wine and honey cakes from the bounty of the King. The girls had brought garlands of wild flowers for the garland dances. All were in their festal dresses.

Now from below came the procession of the two white bulls, the holy beasts for the sacrifice, and behind them many sheep, for a great deal of meat would be required for all those people when the Gods had had their share. At the top of the hill, just beside the altar, fire-pits had been dug, with spits made of pine trees. Here the bulls and sheep would be roasted and the people would dance and sing until the meal was ready.

The white-robed Druids, successors to Ceredig and Syweddyd, with their gold moon-necklets and white head-veils, received the procession at the top of the hill and the sacrifice was made. Some of the Druids, perhaps, who had learnt the old lore by word of mouth, remembered how Brutus of Troy had blessed this spot and hallowed it by the sacrifice of a white bull. And so it was done. But the people waited.

Then, over the edge of the hill, the King appeared, with Rud his brother and Lir his son, and between them they carried the King's kite, the great machine. In vain Rud and Lir had waylaid him and tried to stop him. In the end they could but come with him. Elen, with a little group of her women, remained withdrawn on the outskirts of the crowd. Blaedud hesitated, then ran quickly to her.

"This is nothing, my dear," he said. "Don't look so doomfast. I shall fly a little to amaze the people and be back with you soon enough."

She could not speak, but stretched out her hands to clasp his. He kissed her cold cheek and almost ran from her, violently, as if he dreaded to stay longer.

The machine was ready poised on the lip of the hill. Men-at-arms kept the crowd back, or they would have pressed upon him. Rud helped him, though he needed no ropes now. Smoothly he launched over the edge, soared and was away, up and up into the air. The crowd gasped with wonder and shouted with delight. He could feel their acclamation buoying him up with the current of warm air that carried him.

Up and up, and now he could see below him the dwindling crowd, the pinpoints of the fires, the movement, the smoke, and then further the line of the great river and the town that had grown beside it, with stone houses and paved streets—and there was the white-pillared Temple of the Sun. But still he soared and now he knew the Bird-Woman was beside him. Without turning his head he was conscious of her face bending over him, could feel her soft feathers close against his back and the strong thrust of her wings that carried him forward. He had no fear nor could he think of anything else while she was with him.

The sky was cloudless. No storms, no terrors. There was the level floor of blue and white and then they were through that and into a pale translucent mist. He could hear the Bird-Woman saying, "Come up higher," and somewhere outside—outside what?—he could hear voices saying, "Come up higher, come up higher, and I will show thee things—things that shall be hereafter."

On the white mist around him, pictures began to appear. He seemed to see two men, in unfamiliar clothes, flying in a machine not unlike his own, a great spreading kite, though the shape seemed to change from minute to minute. There was something that drove the kite forward, a little fiery thing made of metal, that blazed and spat and gave off smoke but drove the machine forward against the wind, and a thing like a windmill span rapidly like a dragonfly's wings and cut into the air ahead.

"Oh, that's the thing I wanted!"

The two men and their machine seemed to pass and drop away below. A host of pretty coloured balls came floating up and past, and each of them seemed to have a basket hanging below it, and a man in each one. Then a long slim shape like a fish, silver-coloured, floated grace- fully up alongside of Blaedud. He could see that there were men in the canoe-shaped thing slung underneath it. The mist cleared below and he could see that the great silver fish was floating over cities, larger cities than he ever could have believed. And there were kite-things too, but stronger, neater, more compact, more powerful . . .

He drifted on among them, savouring the wonder, the fulfilment. Then his eye caught movement. The men in the flying-ship were preparing to drop something over, a bag, it seemed, of something heavy. His eye followed it down till it hit the far-off buildings. He heard thunder and all below sprang into flames and fragments. In almost the same moment a kite swooped above the flying ship. There was a rattling sound and the flying ship burst into flames and fell through the air.

Vessel after vessel joined the fight, aircraft after aircraft of different kinds, more and more powerful. Machines crashed down. Below on the ground whole cities burned. He knew there must be men there, and women and children.

"They carry death!" he exclaimed.

"Death?" the Bird-Woman said behind him. "But death is the lot of us all."

He turned half round to see her. "You also?"

"I think I shall be changed," she said.

But now as he looked down the scene was different. The terrors of the airy war seemed to have gone, at least for a time. Aircraft went to and fro now without hindrance—

great smooth things, truly like birds, like giant birds—going from land to land, over lands never heard nor dreamt of, innumerable as bees in and out of their hives on a sunny day.

"What do they carry?" he asked.

"Things and people—men and women to their work and their pleasure, families to meet across the world, lovers to meet and part, enemies to pursue and kill and flay, warriors to fight, scholars to learn, infants to be born, corpses to be buried."

"And things?"

"Oh, wealth and treasures of all kinds—things for beauty, use, comfort, toil, things good and things bad, wisdom and foolishness, toys and mysteries, medicines and diseases, blessings and curses. All of them, more and more, faster and faster, till the world goes mad . . . But look now."

Straight up from the ground, like an arrow indeed, much more like an arrow than ever was Aithro-batés's—a long narrow silver thing that glittered when the light caught it, a vehement fire blazing like lightning under its tail—up it went, straight up.

"Oh, where is it going?" Blaedud gasped.

"Look," she said. "Up there."

Straight up above them was the full moon and there the silver arrow was going. It found its mark away up there. On the very Moon itself men, strange disguised figures, were setting foot.

"Oh," he cried, "they will do it! I always knew they would! Flight, flight, more than any bird—"

"Are you content?"

"I am content, and yet—will they go further? Is there more?"

"Come up higher," she said.

He put out his hands to the controls of the kite, but . . .

"Where is it? The machine?"

"Oh, you will not need it now. It's gone. Neither will you need your body. Come up higher. It's time."

And down below the crowd watched in horror as the machine plunged to earth and crashed, with the spent body, on the roof of the Temple of the Sun.

Lir gathered Elen into his arms and hid her eyes from the sight. And a great sound of wailing and groaning went up from all the tribe.

But above in the sky the larks were singing in the face of the Sun. And beyond them, the Bird-Woman was saying to Blaedud,

"Come up higher."

**"AN AMAZEMENT . . . ENCHANTING
. . . ELECTRIFYING."**
The New York Times

**"MAY BE A CLASSIC FOR READERS
NOT YET BORN."**
Philadelphia Inquirer

"TO READ IT IS TO FLY"
People Magazine

**THE NATIONALLY ACCLAIMED NOVEL BY
WILLIAM WHARTON**